Contents

Meet me at the dance

There once was a witch called Annabel who lived in a small Gloucestershire village called Happy End. This is the story of the village, its characters and Annabel's efforts to help the village and to guide and nurture her daughter Betsy.

Everyone has been brought up on tales of wicked witches as in Snow White and the Seven Dwarfs and The Wizard of Oz, but few people realise that every village, town and city has its own witch. Not necessarily a wicked witch, but a white witch, or a 'wisewoman' as many prefer to be known today.

Annabel was the wisewoman of Happy End and her job was to make sure that everyone in the village was happy and contented. Not an easy task as you might imagine, but being a witch she was very successful. Many of her spells, potions, remedies and treatments had been handed down to her from her mother who in turn had received them from her mother.

Mind you, if you managed to get a look at one of the big books that contained Annabel's notes you would find a lot less eye of newt and tail of frog. These days you would be much more likely to find tarragon vinegar, juice of fennel and so on. Things change and witches like everyone else change with them.

The witch we remember from our childhood is usually a hunched-up, black figure with a pointed chin and very pointed hat. Annabel looked nothing like that. She was a jolly, round-faced, well-built person who looked as though the sun shone eternally out of her very blue eyes. Henry, her husband, unofficial mayor of the village, was also a placid man as people who deal with plants and the land usually are. Henry had been a farmer but in the hard times of the twenty-first century had developed his land on the edge of Happy End into a plant nursery. Since both he and his wife had the green fingers of true gardeners it had been only a short step from arable farming to growing plants, herbs and vegetables for sale to the public. His plant growing was so successful that he had begun to sell to other local garden centres.

* * *

The village of Happy End was the perfect place to live. As its name implied it was at the end of nowhere. That is to say you went from Cirencester on the Barrow Magna road, going left and then turning off right down a narrow lane, keeping going until at the end there was the village. Set in the rolling Cotswold Hills, it was on a wooded slope on the one side and looked across to Barrow Hill on the other where, it was said by some, that the fairies lived.

The view across from the village was spectacular especially in the evening when the setting sun struck obliquely across the village casting long shadows making the fir trees on Barrow Hill stand out proud and tall their blackness silhouetting against the golden sky.

On the day our story begins, Annabel was picking herbs on Barrow Hill. The sun was streaming through the trees and the day felt good. It was springtime and everything was green and fresh. Very often, her daughter Betsy accompanied her, as Betsy loved to dance on Barrow Hill. Dancing with the fairies, she called it. Today Annabel was on her own.

She rested for a moment, looking out across the valley to her village nestling in the fold of the next hill. She could see the vicar, the Reverend Alistair Harding, coming out of the wicket gate of the churchyard saying 'Good morning' to the two elderly sisters Rosemary and Emily Pettit on their way to the Post Office and General Store to buy their groceries. She knew that they were also looking forward to a good gossip with Mrs Garner who kept the store.

Not that there was a lot to gossip about at present. The main topic of conversation was Bill Baxter the local rat catcher and poacher (although no-one had caught him at it

- or if they had they weren't telling). Bill had a smallholding and a field between the village and Barrow Hill. The gossip was that a Bristol businessman had made him an offer to buy the field but Bill and his wife Maureen as yet had not confirmed or denied the rumour.

The vicar got on his bicycle and pedalled past the Post Office on his daily round of visiting the sick and the elderly. Although Annabel was far off on the opposite hill, her view of the village was perfect and she could see everything that was going on. She had trudged up the lane from the village with her basket to pick the wild herbs on the hill feeling the warmth of the sun on her face and arms.

Her husband Henry said she was daft.

'Why don't you take the herbs from my herb collection?' he asked.

What Henry never understood was that although he had an extremely good collection of herbs they were never quite the same as the wild herbs that Annabel picked fresh from the hillside and then made into her medicines and potions before they lost their goodness.

The vicar had disappeared into Mrs Cooke's cottage where her husband was ill in bed.

Annabel had two helpers in the village, The Reverend Alistair Harding who looked after the souls of the villagers, and Dr Julian Everett who looked after their health.

Annabel's work was more subtle than the work done by the other two, she not only helped when people came to her in need, she also adjusted the delicate balance of temperaments and personalities between the people of the village. A little mental nudge here and a tweak there kept everyone happy and content. Sometimes quick emergency measures were needed but not often.

Her eye was caught by a car drawing up to the entrance to Bill Baxter's field down in the valley. Two men got out and went into the field. Annabel looked at them idly but then her attention was caught by the daily bus making its way out of the village heading up the lane towards the main road. As she watched, it swerved violently, stopped and she could see a body lying in front of it.

Witches don't always need broomsticks to get somewhere in a hurry so, in a twinkling of an eye she was at the scene of the accident.

Young Tony Raven lay where he had fallen, his bicycle by his side. Putting her basket on the grass verge she went over and helped him gently to his feet. 'What happened?' asked Annabel although of course, she knew, but she wanted Tony to speak about it.

'I was on my way home, Miss when he came over to my side of the lane and pushed me off my bike.' He looked at Sid Fellows, the driver of the bus, who came hurrying up looking white-faced and shaken.

'Morning, Mrs Witchell,' he said, 'Is the boy all right? I swerved for a rabbit that darted out in front of me. Is he all right?'

Annabel looked Tony up and down. 'Where does it hurt?' she asked.

'I'm all right, Miss,' he said, rubbing his knee. Annabel paused for a moment as though in thought and then said to Sid, 'Yes, he's not hurt. Just a little bruised but no harm done.'

She made sure that his bicycle wasn't damaged and then patted him on his way.

'I ought to report it.' Sid was still looking worried.

'No harm done, Sid, it wasn't your fault. I would leave it be.'

Reassured, Sid went back to his bus in turn talking reassuringly to his five passengers who were just off for a day's shopping in Cirencester and who would be returning that afternoon when the bus made its return trip. Two trips a day, Happy End, around the villages then Cirencester, and back in the morning, the same in the afternoon.

As the bus drove off raising a scurry of dust from the dry surface of the lane Annabel looked round and then stood absolutely still.

'Come out, little bunny,' she called, 'Let's see if you are all right.' She stood half crouching, as motionless as a statue for what seemed an age. Slowly, cautiously, a tiny bewhiskered face peered out of the long grass at the edge of the lane. Soon a tiny body followed bounding up to her outstretched hand and nibbling delicately at the dandelion leaf it found there.

'Why you're only a baby,' Annabel said, 'Go home to your mother and be more careful next time.'

The baby rabbit looked up at her, twitched its whiskers and was gone.

Annabel straightened up, picked up her basket and walked slowly down the lane to the village.

Tony was waiting for her at the bend of the lane, leaning on his bicycle. 'Did you really talk to that rabbit?' he asked as she drew level with him.

'Of course,' said Annabel, 'Don't you talk to your rabbits?'

She knew that Tony's father Jim let him keep three lovely tame white angora rabbits provided he looked after them himself.

'Yes, I do,' said Tony, 'But they be tame uns not wild.'

Annabel gave him a smile and went on down the lane.

Tony called after her, 'Our Lloyd is taking your Betsy to the dance tonight.'

That wasn't strictly true but it was near enough. It was the annual thanksgiving dance that evening and Annabel knew that Jim Raven's eldest son Lloyd had arranged to meet Betsy there. Henry would take her but they were allowing Lloyd to see her home.

As Annabel walked along thinking about her daughter growing up, there was a sudden hurried patter of feet by her side and Emily of the Pettit sisters clutched at her basket.

'I was just coming over to see you. I've sent Rosemary home with the groceries but I had to see you. Can you do anything for my toothache?'

Annabel could see that her right cheek was inflamed and she was obviously in pain. Shifting the basket into her other hand she gently laid the palm of her hand on Emily's cheek. Immediately Emily relaxed as she felt a sense of relief.

'That will ease the pain until we get to the house,' Annabel said. 'Come on.'

Betsy came up out of the garden as they reached the house. 'Can you take the basket, Betsy love? I will deal with it in a minute.'

'Come on into the workshop, my dear,' she said to Emily. She led her to the back of the house where she had her 'den'.

Annabel's den was in an old potting shed, covered on one side with shelves housing all sorts of bottles, jars, dried plants, herbs, mixing bowls, instruments, ladles, an egg timer and books of all shapes and sizes. On the other side of the room a large table was half covered with Annabel's latest experiments. Open in front of them was the large leather-bound spells book in which she recorded her results. She quickly closed it as she came up to the table. On the other end of the table was a surprisingly modern food processor, a coffee grinder and what looked like an electric bread maker.

This was the first time that Emily had been in the den and she looked round in a somewhat dazed fashion. 'Sit down for a moment,' Annabel indicated a chair by the table, then sat down beside her. 'Now let's have a look.'

Annabel could see from the inflamed gum that before anything could be done the swelling had to come down. The nearest dentist was in Cirencester and from the look of the tooth causing the infection it badly needed treatment.

'I can give you a poultice that will clear up the infection,' she said, 'Then you must get to your dentist and let him take a look. It will take a minute to mix up. Just sit there and relax.' She got busy with her pestle and mortar grinding up the ingredients and then added just enough liquid to make it into a paste which she put into a pill box. 'There,' she said, 'That should keep you going. Smear a little on the gum where the infection is night and morning after eating.'

Emily now smiling made to reach into her purse but Annabel waved her away.

'You will be all right now, 'she said, 'But remember get to your dentist as quickly as you can.'

After Emily had gone Betsy came in with the basket. 'Why didn't you do a spell to fix her tooth?' she asked.

'Because,' said Annabel, 'Because, spells are not just to be thrown about and used for everyone and everything. You have to learn control and use them only for important things and good things. Also, spells used for bad purposes can rebound on the sender, always remember that.'

'So Emily's tooth wasn't important enough?' Betsy said.

'Of course it was important, but it was something the dentist could and should fix. The important thing was the pain that she was in and that we needed to fix immediately.'

Betsy sighed 'I suppose I will get the hang of it one day. It's a great responsibility being a witch's daughter.'

'What you need to think about is the dance tonight,' said Annabel. 'You need to look your best for Lloyd.'

Betsy brightened up and gave little twirl as though she were already dressed for the dance. 'I'm going to wear my blue dress. I have just been waiting for the right occasion,' she said.

'That will look lovely with your silver shoes.'

Betsy nodded and bounced out of the room leaving Annabel unpacking the basket of herbs that she had gathered.

After supper Betsy went up to change and came down dressed in her new flowing short-sleeved dress made from soft blue cotton. Annabel looked up at her as she descended the stairs with a feeling of great satisfaction. She was no longer a child, she was a young woman and the feelings of love flowed out towards her.

Although Betsy was only a witch in training she knew exactly what her mother thought and felt and she smiled down at her. 'I love you too, Mum,' she said bounding down the last few steps and throwing herself into her mother's arms.

Henry came out of the living room and she gave a little twirl for both of them. 'There, do I look all right?'

'You look very all right.' Henry looked at Annabel and smiled. 'To think we have such a lovely daughter.'

'Come on, Pa,' Betsy tugged at him. 'You're taking me to the Village Hall. I don't want to be late.'

'Oh all right,' Henry went to put on his coat 'But you don't want to get there too early. You will be there before the boys and you ought to keep them all waiting.'

They had agreed that Betsy would meet Lloyd at the dance but would walk her back afterwards as it was only a short distance to the Church Hall. Lloyd was Betsy's special friend. They had known each other since the time they were allowed to roam the fields and the woods - to Betsy it seemed that they had known each other for ever.

Every year after the corn had been gathered in from the nearby farms and when the autumn fruits decked the Church for Harvest Thanksgiving, the youngsters and some of the oldsters turned out for the annual harvest dance at the Church Hall. Most of the older people in the village preferred to stay at home, putting their feet up with a nice warm fire watching TV or reading a book. Some took the opportunity to get on with their knitting woolly sweaters for winter.

Henry eased himself into his coat while Annabel helped Betsy into her cloak. The cloak was a thick fleecy garment that came right down to her toes and would certainly keep her warm until she reached the hall.

When they arrived Henry stepped in for a moment to wish the vicar 'Good evening' while Betsy left her cloak in the Ladies room. Surprisingly there were quite a few people there already and the small band consisted of piano, drums, bass and guitar were just launching in to a number.

The Church Hall was new this year having been built with a grant from the European Union as had quite a few other Church Halls in villages across the country.

The new building was impressive. It had a large room that could be used for meetings or dances. The raised dais at one end presently occupied by the band could be pushed away into an alcove. It also had proper cloakrooms and toilets. It even had a small room upstairs that was used by the Parochial Church Council for its meetings.

As Henry turned to go Betsy stepped out into the hall,

a slim straight figure. Her golden hair pulled back into two clusters held together by two tinsel bands rescued from last Christmas' decorations.

It seemed to Henry that every eye turned in her direction and some of the girls looked envious when their boyfriends' attention was riveted by the charm and simplicity that she radiated.

He waved to her and then was back in the evening air. As he went out he passed Lloyd going in.

'Bring her back safely,' he called 'Don't be too late.'

Henry noticed Lucy Baxter following closely behind him. She had recently become barmaid at The Fox's Revenge. He shook his head. She'll come to no good, that one, he thought noticing her skimpy dress under a wrap which accentuated her prominent bosom.

He said the same to Annabel when he got back to the house.

Annabel just smiled at him as she put a batch of cakes into the oven. 'Youngsters have to have their fling and there's no harm in the girl.'

That wasn't exactly the thought that was in Betsy's mind at that moment for having seen Lloyd come into the hall with Lucy she waited for him to leave his coat and come over to her. But he didn't come. She saw Lucy leading him over to the corner of the hall where Gladys Brown, who kept the pub The Fox's Revenge with her husband Richard, was dispensing lemonade, orange juice, beer and cakes from a portable bar.

Gladys greeted them with a 'Hallo, Lucy, got a new friend have you? Hallo, Lloyd, you watch that one.'

Gladys was a buxom woman, always cheerful, always speaking her mind but with no intention to harm anyone. 'You should be doing this, Lucy my girl. Poor old Richard is on his own in the pub tonight.'

'Two lemonades, Mrs B,' Lucy pretended she hadn't heard. 'You pay, Lloyd.'

Lloyd looked helplessly across the room at Betsy who just shrugged and turned away to talk to a group of friends.

Although Lucy was a very outward looking girl she had few friends. People who knew her well thought she was too pushy. The only people who didn't know her well were usually casual visitors to The Fox's Revenge and they like a bit of a chat and her flirting behaviour. It was obvious to Lloyd that Lucy had no-one to partner her at the dance and had decided to make him her companion for the evening.

Lloyd handed Lucy her lemonade, put his own down on a side table and said, 'Sorry I have got to go.'

He made his way through the crush to where Betsy was standing. Such a sweet natured patient person, he thought as he came up to her.

Unfortunately he wasn't very good at reading danger signals. If he had been, he would have seen Betsy tapping her feet and tossing her head impatiently.

Fortunately for Lloyd, Betsy needed only one glance to know what had happened and bit back the angry comment that was on her lips. Her training came into action and what she actually said was, 'Poor you. I saw Lucy capture you, but you are safe now,' but she thought if that minx tries to get at you again she will get more than she bargained for!

Several unpleasant spells formed in her mind but she shrugged them away.

Lloyd brightened up considerably and they both began to enjoy the evening.

Old favourites, new favourites, the band seemed to know them all. They played away with pints of beer balanced on the piano. The youngsters in the hall stuck to non-alcoholic drinks but the few oldies went for the beer. It was altogether what a village dance should be.

Before Betsy had left for the dance, Annabel said, 'Keep your eyes open for any awkward or unpleasant situations which might develop and apply a little magic if you need to.'

Betsy was thrilled by this as it was the first time that her mother had asked her to be part of looking after the village and its happiness. She was determined not to let Annabel down. This was her first big assignment.

As it happened not much marred the evening. She spotted old Mr Heathcote who had a bit too much to drink so without interfering with her dancing she gently thought him into the cloakroom where he was helped into his coat by Emily Pettit who, having recovered from her toothache, was acting as cloakroom lady. Before he realised it Betsy had thought him outside and he found himself on his way home.

She began to enjoy herself. Lloyd was normally a rather self-conscious awkward person but with a little thought nudge from Betsy, just a tiny adjustment to his self-confidence and he blossomed into a superb dancer. Circling round the floor they darted in and out of the crowd of dancers. One minute here, the next there circling past Lucy who stood at the edge of the floor with a glass of lemonade in her hand.

The next instant Betsy felt a wet patch spread across the side of her dress as Lucy 'accidentally' split her drink all over her.

Betsy turned to Lucy, her eyes blazing. 'You did that on purpose! Lloyd, wait for me. I will have to try to clean this up.'

Ever helpful Emily Pettit followed her into the Ladies room with a clean towel and helped her to dab the excess liquid off it.

'It's such a lovely dress,' she said, 'but it will mark terribly if you don't soak it in cold water soon. You ought to get home as quickly as possible. Let me get your coat for you and another clean towel.'

Betsy felt wet all over and so taking Emily's advice she slipped her cloak over the wet dress keeping the towel between it and the fabric of the cloak.

Going back into the hall she saw Lloyd looking for her on the other side of the room. Before she could get to him Lucy grabbed him and pulled him on to the dance floor.

This is too much, thought Betsy, and before she could stop herself she put a slippery floor spell on Lucy.

Almost immediately Lucy staggered, clutching at Lloyd to save herself from falling, then as she lost her balance completely, dragged him down with her. As Betsy watched Lloyd got to his feet but Lucy lay moaning on the ground her leg crumpled under her.

Dr Everett was at the bar and seeing Lucy on the ground came over to see what was the matter. He gently probed her ankle. 'You are lucky,' he told her, 'A slight sprain but you will be right as rain in a couple of days.'

'Couple of days?' Lucy wailed.

'First we must get you home,' he said. 'I have my car outside. Will you help me, Lloyd?'

They helped her to get to her feet, then, with her arm round Lloyd's shoulders she hobbled to the cloakroom where they got their coats and went out to the car which Dr Everett had driven up to the door.

Lloyd was too preoccupied to notice Betsy as he thought that what had happened was his fault. Betsy just stood feeling wet all over unable to think of anything.

As Lloyd and Lucy left the hall a small voice in her head said, 'Serve you right, now you will have to go home on your own.'

It wasn't very far from the hall to home so Betsy drew her cloak around her and headed for the door. As she went out a figure stepped out from the shadow of the porch and at first she thought it was Lloyd, but it was her father. 'Oh,

Pa, I'm glad you are here. I'm so wet and miserable, can we go home?'

'That's what I'm here for,' said Henry. 'Your mother thought you might need a little help, so here I am.'

Later, safely back at home after a hot bath with Annabel putting her dress to soak in cold water, she sat in the big chair by the fire clad in her warm floral patterned pyjamas, her knees drawn up to her chin. Henry sat in the chair opposite and Annabel settled on the settee with her knitting.

'Oh, Mum. It was terrible, that Lucy making it so obvious that she wanted Lloyd and then me getting all wet. I couldn't help what I did to her but it all went wrong,' and she burst into tears completely wetting the handkerchief that Annabel held out to her.

'Two wrongs don't make a right,' said Annabel draping the handkerchief over the fireguard where it began to steam the tears away. 'You will have to learn to control yourself a bit better.'

'But, Mum, she spilled her drink over me deliberately, I couldn't help myself.'

'And you saw where it got you,' said Annabel. 'Because of your actions you lost Lloyd and would have had to see yourself home if I hadn't sent your Pa to meet you. Evil acts have a habit of rebounding on the sender and you must remember that our job is to help people not to harm them.'

'But, Mum.' Betsy turned her big blue eyes opened wide looking at her mother.

'No buts,' said Annabel firmly. 'You did a good job sending Mr Heathcote home, but you hurt Lucy and it took Lloyd away from you. Fortunately there is no permanent damage and next time you will remember to be more careful.'

'Thanks, Mum, I'm going up to bed now. Good night.' She kissed them both and scampered up the stairs.

2

Love All

Betsy sat on the edge of the table watching her mother make up a Feverfew remedy for rheumatism.

'It's a good mixture to relieve the pain,' Annabel said. 'I'm making this up for old Mrs Twitchett, the old lady down at the end of the village. She suffers terribly from her rheumatics. This is a tincture made from the fresh leaves I collected this morning.'

Betsy was just back from school in Barrow Magna where she was in the sixth form. She would soon be taking her exams and hoping to go to university. In addition to her studies she took every opportunity she could to learn from her mother so that she could follow in her footsteps.

At the moment all seemed well with the village except for the new houses that had just been built on the field above the school. A developer had bought the piece of land opposite the church just above the Infant and Junior School where Miss Tatt was Head Teacher. He had managed to cram six houses into the space.

They were so close that they only had very small gardens front and back. The Estate Agent Donald Tanner from Barrow Magna said that people who were working in either Barrow Magna or Cirencester and commuting every day would have no time for gardens. This, as Annabel remarked to Henry, was a very male perspective as it neglected the fact that their wives would be stuck in the house with little or no garden for their children to play in.

Everyone in the village was very apprehensive about the people that would come to 'disturb our little community.' Their fears were justified as the first person to come was Mr George Griffiths, his wife Griselda and young son Tommy.

They took the house nearest to the school so that Tommy only had to hop out of the gate and in through the back entrance to be in the school in a matter of minutes.

Tommy was a normal healthy young boy, but his parents were definitely different. Griselda, his mother, was soon seen in the village stores dressed in what the village thought were very unsuitable clothes, a vivid red mini skirt and a white T-shirt with the words 'Imbas Forosnal' blazoned across her chest.

Betsy had to go and look up the wording in the library discovering it in a book on Celtic mythology with the meaning 'having a special gift for clairvoyance.'

When she reported this to her mother, Annabel was quite concerned.

'She sounds like one of these modern dabblers in witchcraft,' she said. 'Mark my words no good will come of it if she is.'

It wasn't only Griselda Griffiths who appeared to be a problem. George Griffiths promised to be an even worse one. He was short, fat and pompous, just retired from a job in Gloucester and wanting to move to a more rural setting. However, retirement seemed to be the last thing in his mind for no sooner had he settled into his new house than he began to make himself felt in the village and indeed beyond. No-one knew how he got himself on the local Parish Council but he did and it was Counsellor Griffiths this and Counsellor Griffiths that afterwards.

Some said that he had a brother on the Council but people always say things like that and since there was no-one called Griffiths on the Council until he arrived nothing was proved. It did mean that he poked his nose into everything, telling the vicar how to run his services and going to the local parent/teacher association telling Miss Tatt how to teach her children more efficiently.

The rest of the houses gradually filled up but the inhabitants were mainly quiet ordinary people compared with the Griffiths menagerie.

The first real indication of trouble came when Emily Pettit found Lucy Baxter sobbing her heart out on a bench outside the local pub, the Fox's Revenge. Lucy had the job of barmaid at the pub.

'What's the matter, Lucy my love?' she asked.

Between sobs Lucy told her that Lloyd Raven had refused to go out with her.

'I thought Lloyd was a special friend of Betsy Witchell?' she said.

'Lloyd likes me, I know.' Lucy ignored what Emily had said and went on, 'and I'm going to do something about it.'

Emily thought no more about it until she heard that Lucy had gone up to the new houses to see Griselda Griffiths. This intelligence was from Eva Raven who did cleaning for a number of houses in the village and had been seized on as soon as the Griffiths got to Happy End.

'You should see what Mrs G has got in her spare room,' she said. 'Laid out like a witch's den it is. Not like Annabel's place of course, but she is obviously up to some sort of witchery.'

'What did Lucy want with her?' asked Emily.

'That I don't know,' said Eva after Emily had told her about her encounter with Lucy. 'If it's anything to do with our Lloyd then that Lucy had better watch out.'

'I think you ought to tell Annabel about this especially if witching is concerned.'

Annabel listened carefully to Eva's account both of the spare room and Lucy's visit.

Meanwhile Lucy had taken the small bottle that Griselda had given her and was trying to work out how to get Lloyd to drink it.

'It's a love potion,' Griselda told her. 'A few drops of this and he won't be able to resist you.'

As Lucy served in the pub the easiest way would be to spike his drink but he never came into the Fox's Revenge. How could she get him to come?

Lucy wasn't a particularly bright girl but once she got an idea in her head it was very difficult to get it out.

Days went by and nothing happened but then one day she met Lloyd outside the pub. He had just started working for Henry at the Garden Centre and was on his bicycle delivering plants round the village. His next port of call was Miss Tatt up at the school but it was a hot day and when Lucy invited him in for a drink, he accepted.

'Just lemonade,' he said. 'I'll stay outside if you don't mind.' He sat on the bench while Lucy went in and came back with two glasses of sparkling lemonade.

In stories, the person putting the love potion in someone's drink always ends up getting the wrong glass but as there was only the two of them Lloyd got the right glass and drank it down gratefully.

'Thanks, Lucy. I must be off,' he said and off he went.

'That isn't how it is supposed to happen,' thought Lucy.' I suppose I can wait.'

What she didn't realise was that love potions don't work immediately but take a little while to get into the system. She should have kept Lloyd there for at least ten minutes.

The result was that when he got to the school and delivered the plants to Miss Tatt the potion began to work.

Miss Tatt was about to go into class when Lloyd called and after thanking him for the plants she turned to go. Lloyd just stood there staring at her.

'Thank you, Lloyd, you can go now,' she said sharply.

Lloyd took a step forward and looked as if he was going to embrace her. 'Miss Tatt, I ...' then getting a grip on himself he said, 'Thank you, Miss Tatt. Is there anything else I can do for you?'

Miss Tatt took a step backwards and looked flustered.

'No, thank you, Lloyd, goodbye.' She turned and scuttled into the classroom.

He stood there for a minute and then slowly got on his bicycle and rode away.

'I don't know what's wrong with him,' Eva said to her husband next day when he got home from work.

'Lloyd's not usually like this. He's been mooning around the house all day muttering something about needing to go back to school.'

Jim Raven took his boots off and said, 'Maybe the lad's sickening for something. Why don't you have a word with Annabel Witchell? See if she can do something for him.'

Next day Eva went over to see Annabel after she had finished her cleaning.

'I think Griselda Griffiths has been giving Lucy some sort of potion,' she said. 'Lucy was up there again today asking for another dose as the first one didn't work.'

She then told Annabel about Lloyd's strange behaviour.

'Yesterday he went up to his bedroom and got out all his

old school exercise books. You know the one's where Miss Tatt makes them write essays and then corrects them. Today he said he's going up to talk to Miss Tatt after work. He wants to go back to school. I don't know what's going on.'

One thing witches can do is put two and two together so it wasn't hard to explain Lloyd's behaviour in terms of Lucy's visit to the Griffiths household.

'Lucy is up to something with Lloyd Raven,' she told her husband later that day. 'She has always fancied him after that episode at the dance but what Miss Tatt has got to do with it I have no idea. I'll have a word with him when he comes in for work in the morning.'

Next morning just as Lloyd was reporting for work, Annabel came out of the house and into the plant centre.

'Why hello, Lloyd,' she said, then to her husband, 'Can you spare him for a minute. I want to ask him a thing or two up at the house.'

Henry who had already been primed for this shrugged and said, 'Get back as soon as you can, we've a lot to do today.'

Back at the house Annabel sat Lloyd down and said, 'What's this I hear about you wanting to go back to school? You've got a good job here with Henry so what's it all about?'

Lloyd looked white-faced but said very clearly, 'I want to be near Miss Tatt. You see I love her.'

Annabel was taken aback but suddenly two and two made four.

'Have you been in touch with Lucy recently?' she asked.

'Not really,' said Lloyd. 'I did see her at the pub the other day but that's all.'

It took some time but Annabel eventually extracted the whole story about the glass of lemonade, the visit to Miss Tatt and how Lloyd fell in love with her.

She reported back to Henry and Betsy that night.

'It looks as though Griselda Griffiths gave Lucy a potion to bind Lloyd to her but forgot to tell her that it takes about ten minutes to work. That's what comes of amateurs meddling in witches' business.'

'What's going to happen, Mum?' asked Betsy. 'Lloyd is my friend and I want him back.'

'I've already given him the antidote so he is cured of Miss Tatt and I don't think she has been inconvenienced so she is best left alone. What we must do now is concentrate on the problem as it looks as if Lucy is going to try again. Eva said that she has got another dose of the same stuff.'

Next afternoon Lucy was behind the bar at the Fox's Revenge washing glasses. No-one much came in until later so she was surprised to see Annabel come through the door.

'Hello, Lucy,' Annabel sat down heavily on one of the bar stools. 'I'm fair puffed. Do you mind if I sit down for a minute?'

'Of course not, Mrs Witchell. Shall I call Mr Brown?'

'No, that's fine but I would appreciate a glass of water.'

'Of course,' Lucy said, 'I'll pour you one. Are you sure you wouldn't like something else?'

'Well, since you mention it, dear, how about joining me in a nice glass of lemonade?'

Lucy poured two glasses, set them on the bar and came round the bar to sit with Annabel. As she came round the bar Annabel quickly poured the contents of a small bottle into one of the glasses. Taking one glass in her hand, she handed Lucy the other doctored glass.

Raising her glass she said, 'Thanks for helping an old woman, Lucy. Actually you could help me even more. I'm so whacked out today and I was supposed to deliver this letter to the Griffiths' house. Would you be very kind and slip up there with it for me?'

Lucy had been wondering how she could get another word with Griselda Griffiths to ask how she could get Lloyd to drink the new potion so this suited her very well.

'I'm sure Mr Brown wouldn't mind me doing that for you,' she said. 'I'll just go and ask him as he will have to mind the pub while I'm out.'

Richard Brown came in at that moment and Lucy explained.

'Hello, Annabel,' he said. 'We don't often see you in here. Yes, of course, Lucy, off you go.'

Lucy drank about half the glass of lemonade, took the letter, which actually just contained one of Henry's plant catalogues, and set off.

Richard sat down beside Annabel.

'What's this all about?' he asked. 'You're up to something.'

'You know me too well, Richard Brown,' she said and

settled down to tell him the whole story.

Lucy reached the Griffiths' house and there in the small front garden was George Griffiths fussing over some plants that had obviously been dug up by an animal.

'Dratted cats,' he said. 'Can't leave anything alone. Oh, hello, Lucy are you here to see Griselda?'

'I would like to see her but this is for you,' she said and leaning forward gave him the letter and kissed him on the cheek.

He started back. 'Why, Lucy,' he said.

To his surprise she then put her arms around him and hugged him to her ample bosom.

He struggled to get free.

'Griselda, Griselda come quickly,' he yelled.

His wife looked out of the window in time to see him struggling in Lucy's arms. She was out of the front door in a flash.

'Come inside at once,' she commanded. 'We don't want the neighbours to see this disgusting exhibition.'

She pulled them roughly into the house, Lucy still clutching Mr Griffiths tightly.

*　*　*

'What happened next we shall never know,' laughed Annabel. 'But I think it will teach both Griselda and Lucy a lesson they are not going to forget for a while.'

3

Varley's Field

Their black cat, Ciaran, which had been stretched out in front of the fire, got up, arched its back and strolled off in the direction of the front door.

'It's Bill come to talk about selling his field.' Annabel went to the door.

Even though they had been married for 25 years, Henry still found Annabel's powers a bit overwhelming.

'Evening, Bill.'

'Evening, Henry, Mrs H.'

Bill Baxter was a short stocky man built for the outdoors. As always he entered the house taking his cap off and wiping his boots carefully on the outside mat.

'Sit yourself down, Bill and tell us what we can do for you.' Annabel resumed her seat and picked up her knitting.

'Well it's like this, 'Bill faltered 'I'm beginning to think

I may have made a mistake and I'd like your advice.' He looked appealingly at them both scratching the top of his head disturbing the few wisps of hair left to him.

Annabel and Henry sat back and waited for him to go on.

'You see I've sold my field down in the valley to a chap from Bristol, a Mr Varley, and I don't think he has been playing straight with me.' He stopped and waited for their reaction.

Annabel sat forward. 'Go on,' she commanded. 'Let's hear it all.'

'Well this chap said he wanted to have a nature reserve for ducks and other birds down in my field. Flood it with water he said and it would make the perfect place. What he didn't say was that it would draw tourists, but I thought it would be a good thing. Help the pub, help Henry sell his plants, and even old Smithy at the forge. People might want to buy his wrought iron stuff.'

'You ought to have told the village before you did it, Bill.' Annabel looked sharply at him. 'But of course it's too late now because you have done it.'

'That's not all,' said Bill looking very distressed. 'There's worse to come.'

'What's worse than that?' Henry was alarmed at the prospect of the village becoming a tourist attraction.

Bill looked as if he was going to burst into tears. 'He deceived me, that's what he did. Do you know what happened this morning?'

Annabel and Henry shook their heads.

'This morning two men arrived in a car and started measuring.'

'Measuring?' they echoed.

'Measuring,' he said. 'And what were they measuring, just bases for houses. It all came out. They told me that he was going to build twenty houses on the site. His story about a nature reserve was a lie.'

'But,' Annabel pointed out, 'He can't do it without Council permission. They have to notify us and give us a chance to object.'

'I know,' said Bill, 'but when I met him he boasted that he had a cousin in the housing department who would see his project through, but of course I thought he was talking about a nature reserve.'

'Next time you do something like this at least tell me before it happens.' Henry was the unofficial mayor of the village and most village business was conducted through him.

'I just wanted to sell my field and thought that there was no harm in it, but twenty houses, it will ruin the village it's bad enough having that modern housing estate up the hill.'

Annabel put her knitting down and tapped Bill on the knee with a knitting needle. 'You have been silly, Bill, but don't worry, it will never happen.' She spoke with complete certainty. 'Meet me down at the field at eight o clock in the morning. I will have some questions for you.'

After Bill had gone, she said to Henry, 'Why do they always come to us after the damage has been done? It would have been much easier the other way, now I shall have to think this out very carefully.'

Annabel stayed up quite late, looking through what she called her reference books. They were large leather-bound books full of the writings of her grandmother, her mother and now her own experiments. One was a spells' book, the second was a herbal remedies' book, and the third was what she called her 'situations' book which contained anything that didn't go into the other two.

'I think,' she said to herself, 'this is going to need a special sort of help and I know just where to get it.'

It was past midnight when she closed the situations book, turned out the light and went off to bed. Henry was snoring contentedly as she snuggled under the warm bedclothes going fast asleep straight away.

* * *

Next morning she was up and breakfasted almost before the sun had risen and was off to the field. At eight o clock on the dot Bill Baxter arrived.

Bill found Annabel already there bending over the stream that flowed through the corner of the field.

'Nice clear water,' she said looking up.

'Arrh,' said Bill, 'Used to catch tiddlers in there when I was a boy.'

'Those were the days,' she straightened up and sat on a fallen tree trunk.

She patted the trunk, 'Come and sit beside me, Bill, I've got some questions for you.'

They talked for quite a while until Annabel got up and said, 'Well I will see you later, Bill. I've got lots of things to do this morning.'

'But what's going to happen to the field?' he asked.

'Don't worry,' said Annabel. 'I'm off to see someone who, I hope, will sort this out for us.'

Bill had to be content with this as Annabel strode off in the direction of Barrow Hill.

* * *

When Henry came down that morning he found Betsy making breakfast.

'Where's your Mum?' he asked.

Betsy popped bread into the toaster. 'Gone down to the field,' she said. 'Said she was going to meet Bill Baxter.'

'Well she was up late last night so I suppose she's got some scheme in her head. I don't know exactly what she's up to but whatever it is it won't be good for Mr Varley.'

* * *

Now that she had talked to Bill, Annabel wasted no more time, for she was off to see the fairies.

All the locals knew that fairies lived in Barrow Hill and some claimed to have seen them but no-one could actually prove anything.

Annabel however, not only knew they were there, she knew how to contact them. Her situations book gave detailed instructions.

She had only done this once before when she had saved the life of a fairy that had been caught accidentally by a fox. This had earned her the gratitude of the Fairy Queen who had said that if ever help was needed she was to come to them.

Making her way up the hill with the sun just rising over the top, she went to a group of trees just off the track on the left hand side. There she bent down under a hawthorn bush and groped in what looked like a rabbit hole. Inside she found a small bell which she proceeded to ring.

It rang with a clear penetrating note. Putting the bell back in the hole, Annabel stood back and waited.

After some minutes Annabel could sense the presence of unseen watchers, then as she waited, a whole section of the hillside opened up and what seemed to be a horde of fairies poured out, surrounded her and swept her into the hill.

Fairies are not as small as some people picture them. They are about the height of young children and, unless flying, keep their wings folded behind them.

Annabel found herself in a wide tunnel but before she was able to take much account of her surroundings the hillside closed up on them and she was taken down the tunnel which was lit by fairy lanterns. As they went deeper into the hill Annabel found herself stooping to get through the low tunnels. At last, they reached what must have been the centre of the hill where it widened out into a large cavern.

She couldn't see how it was lit but it was as bright as day. It was like a town in miniature with rows of little houses and shops grouped round a castle set in its own grounds. Annabel was taken along the narrow streets until she came to the grounds of the castle, there she entered an orchard which contained trees of apple, pear, plums and all sorts of fruit. She then walked along a path between vegetable beds with beans and carrots, peas and potatoes, lettuce and tomatoes, all varieties of vegetables and bushes of raspberries, loganberries, gooseberries and other fruits. There was a stream in the garden and fairies were using it to water the plants.

The fairies crowded round her and ushered her into a courtyard leading to the fairy castle. Entering the castle, she was quickly conducted into the Fairy Queen's presence.

The hall in which the .Fairy Queen sat was richly decorated with gold and silver tapestries, the arched ceiling disappeared up into the darkness. The main body of the fairies had left Annabel at the door but she was accompanied by two obviously special fairies dressed in white and gold robes. The Queen waved them away, got up and beckoned Annabel to a seating area in an alcove at the side of the hall.

'You have come about the field I suppose?' she asked.

There was no need for Annabel to show surprise as fairy

powers were greater than her own and they would already have known about the purchase of the field.

'Yes,' she said, 'This silly man Varley thinks he can build houses at the foot of the hill. Something that I am sure you cannot allow.'

'Quite right,' the Fairy Queen replied. 'The village itself is close enough to our domain. If anyone built closer it would be encroaching on our territory. Already we see that new houses have been built at the top of the village but down at the foot of the hill we shall always stop such development.'

'Some of the people in the new houses are already a problem to us,' said Annabel. 'One in particular, a Mr Griffiths, is a pain in our sides but I didn't come to talk about him. What do you think we should do about this new threat?'

They talked on for a while and came to what Annabel thought was a very satisfactory conclusion. Leaving the Fairy Queen she was escorted back up the tunnels and out onto the hillside.

The change from the secret world beneath the hill to the sound of wind in the trees, the clouds running across the sky, the sunlight and the birds singing in the trees was almost magical in itself.

Making her way back home Annabel turned the plan over in her mind and found it almost foolproof. Look out, Mr Varley, she thought.

*   *   *

Although, as far as the village knew, Mr Varley hadn't got planning permission for the houses, there were soon men surveying the site, sticking poles in all over the place and measuring distances. Mr Varley came down every day to watch them at work. He became a very familiar sight in the village arriving early each morning in what the village called his 'super deluxe' car.

Annabel merely sat tight doing nothing except smiling quietly to herself. Then it was the turn of the bulldozers. One morning soon after Annabel's visit to the fairies they came lumbering down the lane heading for Varley's field.

This was too good an opportunity for Annabel to miss as she enjoyed working with machinery. The drivers of the two bulldozers suddenly lost control; their vehicles went at high speed into the field and began careering about in a way that could only be described as dancing. The drivers couldn't stop them as Annabel made them roll up and down, wave their scoops in the air, and stand up as though begging, rock from side to side and generally behaving in a totally erratic fashion. The noise of the engines was terrific and could be heard all over the village drawing the villagers out to see the spectacle.

Mr Varley arrived in his car scattering the villagers as he honked his horn and drove onwards towards the field. As soon as she saw him coming Annabel stopped the spell but kept an engine failure spell on them leaving the two large beasts stranded in the middle of the field.

With the show obviously over everyone headed back to

their houses with smiles on their faces while Mr Varley went angrily up to the drivers who were scratching their heads over what had happened.

'What do you think you are doing?' he asked.

'We don't rightly know, governor,' said Fred, the larger of the two. 'One minute we were coming quietly down the hill and the next minute we were racing all over the field as though we were at an Agricultural Show.'

'Well, stop playing about and get a move on flattening this field.'

Both drivers tried to start their engines but couldn't. Annabel knew that the spell would only last for one hour but that would be enough to hold them up.

'They won't start, governor.' Fred looked across at his mate.

'Well, get someone from the garage to come out and fix them,' said Mr Varley.

Fred pulled out his mobile phone and after a long conversation he called over, 'He says he can't get here until tomorrow.'

'Well take a look at it yourselves. See if you can fix it.' Mr Varley was going red in the face. He went over to his car and thumped hard on the steering wheel.

After several more attempts Fred gave up and went over to help his mate Charlie but the same thing happened.

Charlie turned to Fred and said, 'This ain't no use, Fred, I'm going back to the office, there's a bus around in the next ten minutes.' So leaving Mr Varley fuming they went back up to the bus stop and were soon disappearing into the distance in Sid Fellow's bus.

Mr Varley went over to one of the bulldozers, gave it a poke and then turned back to his car and drove off. All day the machines lay quietly in the field while the village went about its business.

'Time to put plan B into operation tonight,' said Annabel.

Plan B involved quite a lot of coordinated effort between Annabel, aided by Betsy, the fairies and Henry. The day appeared to go quietly on its way but under Barrow Hill the fairies were busy diverting an underground stream with the help of the elves who also inhabited the hill. Henry had gone off on a mysterious errand for Annabel and she and Betsy were busy laying plans to kidnap Mr Varley from his hotel in Cirencester.

That night Mr Varley dreamt that he was sitting on a broomstick behind a witch, flying through the air. He was in his pyjamas and the air wafted all about him. It wasn't unpleasant but it felt very unreal.

Annabel on the other hand, who was piloting the broomstick, was having considerable difficulty as Mr Varley kept sliding over to one side and she kept having to compensate for this.

At last they arrived at their destination and with the help of Henry and Betsy, Mr Varley was safely stowed away for the night. He snuggled down on the pillow they had provided and Annabel drew a blanket over him.

'He's going to get a shock in the morning,' she said quietly to Betsy.

The moon cast its silvery beams on Mr Varley gently snoring in the middle of his field only it was a field no longer.

The next morning word had gone round and there was already a crowd of people standing at the edge of what had been Varley's field.

The word had been spread by Tony Raven, who, delivering papers as usual before he went to school had passed by the field only to find that it wasn't there any more. With a few 'Cor's' and 'Lummes' he abandoned his paper round and went back to tell Mrs Garner at the Post Office Stores.

She was soon on the phone to one or two special cronies and the news spread. Someone even phoned the local TV station, Westerum TV and a reporter and cameraman were hastily dispatched. When they arrived at the village in a noisy van containing their equipment, the scene of the excitement was not hard to find.

Of Varley's field there was no trace. Instead there was a sheet of water with ducks swimming about.

In the middle of this large pond there was a small boat in which could be seen a figure in pyjamas waving its arms about and occasionally stooping down. Further back, the tops of two bulldozers stuck forlornly out of the water.

It was a beautiful morning and Mr Varley's cries could be clearly heard across the water. The TV cameraman had a close-up view of the figure in the boat as it appeared to be trying to bail water out with its bare hands.

Some words could be heard.

'The boat is sinking and I can't swim.'

'Help, Help.'

'Someone please rescue me.'

The crowd parted as Annabel pushed her way through. She could put on a loud and penetrating voice when she needed to.

'What's all this, Mr Varley?' she called. 'You told Bill Baxter that you wanted to turn the field into a water park and now you've got it, so what's wrong?'

The cameraman standing next to Annabel grinned at her. 'This will make a great story for tonight's news broadcast but you can't let him drown. How will you save him?'

'I will tell you later,' said Annabel quietly.

Meanwhile, Mr Varley had given up his feeble attempts to bail out the water and was sitting dejectedly in the boat. 'Help me, someone. I will give anything for someone to rescue me.'

'Anything?' called Annabel.

Mr Varley got up unsteadily. The boat was obviously filling up with water. 'Yes, anything, only help me.'

'How about giving Bill the deeds to his field back?' Annabel called.

'Yes, yes, anything.' Mr Varley stumbled and the boat rocked. 'Only hurry, hurry.'

'Right,' said Annabel. 'Henry to the rescue.'

Henry appeared clad in long wading boots and strode

out purposefully to the centre of the field. The crowd gasped and then began to laugh. The water only came up to the top of Henry's waders. Henry lifted Mr Varley as though he was a feather and carried him back to shore,

The crowd parted to let them through.

Back on dry land clad only in wet pyjamas, a shivering Mr Varley shook his fist at Annabel and said, 'You tricked me. You haven't heard the last of this.'

'I hope not,' said Annabel. 'You promised Bill Baxter his field back.'

Varley stamped angrily on the ground. 'Well he won't get it and as soon as I get this water drained off my land I will have these houses built quicker than you can turn round.'

Annabel caught him by the shoulder. 'Jack Varley,' she said. 'You are a wicked man, but you will keep your promise to hand the deeds back.'

'Huh,' said Varley. 'And who is going to stop me? I shall just deny every word.'

'You can't do that,' said Annabel pointing to the TV cameraman. 'We have everything you said on film and tonight, if I am not mistaken it will be on National TV so you don't have a leg to stand on.'

Mr Varley, a pitiful figure, sagged back against the wall of Bill Baxter's pig house, his pyjamas wet through, his feet deep in rich smelling pig effluent. 'All right, all right, just get me out of here.'

Annabel took pity on the cowering figure and beckoned Henry over. 'You will have to wash his feet first but then put him in the truck and get him back to the hotel.'

Henry, as always, obeyed his wife and first dunking Mr Varley's feet in the water trough, loaded him into the truck and set off for Cirencester. The crowd parted to let them through, still laughing at the comic episode. The TV cameraman and reporter thanked Annabel for letting them in on what they called 'a scoop' and set off in their noisy van.

*　*　*

That night Henry, Annabel and Betsy were gathered round the television.

'Well, it didn't make the National news, but it certainly made the local.' said Annabel. 'I don't think we shall see much of Mr Varley for a long while.'

And they all smiled as Mr Varley's terror-stricken face came up on the screen.

Herbal Remedies

Varley's field had gone back to normal. The fairies had unblocked the underground stream and the water had seeped away, leaving two bedraggled bulldozers that were eventually rescued by the firm that owned them, using a large breakdown truck.

In addition to handing the deeds of the field back to Bill Baxter, which he did without asking for his money back, Mr Varley had to pay quite a large bill for the rescue and reconditioning of the bulldozers – being stuck in water and mud tends not to help engines or machinery.

Although the field eventually dried out and Bill Baxter was able to put his goat, Billie, on the field again, the stream that flowed through one corner of the field had now swollen into a small pond and was loved by the ducks that waded in it. Everything turned out quite well as soon after that an artist, improbably named Tommy Tucker, came to the village. He turned up in the Fox's Revenge one day asking if they knew anywhere that he could park his caravan. Varley's field was the obvious place. Bill Baxter was delighted to let him do that and to collect the small but regular rent he was willing to pay.

Meanwhile, Annabel was busy picking herbs and making them into various remedies ready for what she described as 'the summer rush'.

Every week Henry had a stall at the Saturday market in Barrow Magna, the town just over the hill from Happy End. Here he sold the plants, trees and vegetables that he grew in his garden centre.

Annabel was very excited as Henry had suggested that she might take one end of his stall to display and sell her herbal remedies. She was nervous at first as up to now she had only sold or mostly given away her remedies to people in the village. Henry however said that this was a good opportunity for her to help more people.

Annabel had often helped Henry with his stall and loved the feel and sound of the market. The stallholders calling their wares, the people moving about looking, poking, choosing and sometimes buying everything from cheese to kitchenware and clothing.

The first week she took one end of his stall it was a great success as there was an almost continuous stream of women wanting to buy one remedy or another. This went on for several weeks.

As they were loading the things left over into the truck late one Saturday afternoon, Henry said, 'You know, Annabel, you really ought to get a stall of your own; you get so many customers.'

'You're not jealous, are you?' She turned and looked at him.

'No, not jealous,' he said, 'but you get so many customers and I hardly get any in comparison. Your customers might be stopping people who want to come to my end of the stall because of the activity at your end.'

'Go on,' said Annabel nudging him with her elbow. 'You know as well as I do that a lot of my ladies stop at your end to buy a plant after coming to me.'

'That's true enough,' said Henry, carefully putting a tall apple tree to one side in the truck.

As they were talking and putting things away Annabel became aware of a man standing listening to them.

'Can I do anything to help?' she asked politely.

The man came forward, coughed and said, 'Well, yes I think you can. You see my name is Longbridge, George Longbridge and I own Longbridge's Health Food Shop in the High Street. I wonder if I could talk to you for a minute.'

'Course you can. Can you finish off, Henry, while I talk to this gentleman?' Henry nodded as best he could his chin buried in the large box bush he was carrying.

'Well now and what can I do for you,' she asked.

He straightened his tie, smoothed down his jacket and

said nervously, 'I wonder if you would allow me to sell your herbal remedies in my shop?'

'Well that's an idea,' said Annabel. 'Did you hear that, Henry? Mr Longbridge wants to sell my remedies in his shop. That would solve your problem, wouldn't it?'

'Of course,' said Mr Longbridge hurriedly, 'We would have to work out a proper arrangement, prices, profit and all that sort of thing.'

'Why don't you come over to see me in Happy End,' said Annabel, 'I'm sure we can work something out. Tomorrow's Sunday but you could come over for a cup of tea about three o'clock if that would suit you.'

'That would be fine,' said Mr Longbridge. 'I'll be there and I will bring a proposition for you.'

'We are the house on the side of the garden centre in the village. You can't miss us. See you then.' Annabel waved as he set off back to his shop.

She was full of the idea as they drove back. 'What do you think of that, Henry? Instead of just selling my remedies on a Saturday, they will be on sale six days a week...' She basked in a happy glow all the way home.

Three o'clock on Sunday came and with it Mr Longbridge. Over tea he outlined his proposal. Everything seemed fine except that Annabel wasn't happy about the way he intended to promote her remedies.

'Granny Witchell's Remedies does have a ring about it,' admitted Annabel, 'but I'm not a granny and your picture of a witch stirring a cauldron certainly can't be used. What would people who know me think?'

Eventually they settled on Witchell's Herbal Remedies and Mr Longbridge agreed to cut out the picture of the witch. The arrangement was that Annabel would make, bottle or package the remedies and Mr Longbridge would get 15% of the profit on the sales. He also agreed to set the price for each item.

What Annabel hadn't realised was that instead of using old lemonade bottles and tying up her herbs in brown paper and string, she now had to think about more respectable packaging.

Fortunately Henry knew a supplier of the bottles that chemists use to dispense their medicines and he was able to get her a hundred 100ml bottles at a reasonable price. After thinking about the packaging for the dried herbs they decided to stick to brown paper, but contacted John Perry, the local printers in Barrow Magna to make labels for the various products.

Betsy was brought in to help and Annabel's den began to look like a factory production line.

Three weeks passed before Annabel had a supply of remedies to take to Mr Longbridge's shop. In the meantime she put a notice on Henry's stall every Saturday to say that in a few weeks time her remedies would be sold at the Health Food shop in the High Street.

Mr Longbridge, who had now become George, welcomed them when they brought the first consignment to him. He showed them a poster he had prepared for his window. This time instead of a witch, it showed a rosy-faced country woman holding up a package with one of Annabel's labels on it saying: 'Witchell's Genuine Herbal Remedies'.

'How did you manage that?' asked Annabel in amazement. 'I didn't give you any labels.'

'Ah, well you see, Annabel, I'm a friend of John Perry's and he ran a few extra labels off for me for show.'

'Well, here you are then.' They handed over the boxes of remedies. 'Good luck and let us know how you get on.'

The next week was quite nerve racking for Annabel as she wondered what was happening at Longbridge's shop. She was so fidgety that by Tuesday Betsy said, 'Why don't you go over to Barrow, Mum and see how things are going. I'll come with you if you like.'

'No, I don't want to disturb the man. He's only been at it for a few days. Maybe we can go over with Henry on Saturday. I'll take a look then.'

So they did and while Henry was on his stall they went down to the shop where in the window there was a large sign that said: 'We now sell Witchell's Secret Remedies for All Ills.'

'Secret they may be,' said Annabel, 'but they certainly don't cure all ills. That's false advertising.'

'What are you going to do about it, Mum?' asked Betsy.

'At the moment nothing,' said Annabel, 'but I reckon we will need to keep an eye on this.'

Annabel noticed quite a queue of women in the shop

waiting to be served so it looked as though it was working and had freed her from being on the market stall all the time.

The next week a cheque arrived from George Longbridge with a statement showing how much he had sold and how much percentage he had taken from the profit.

In the accompanying letter he asked Annabel to supply more of each item.

'This looks good,' said Henry.

'Yes,' said Annabel. 'But Betsy and I are going to have to work something out between us as if it goes on at this rate I shall run out of herbs and you can only pick them at special seasons of the year.'

'That's just an old wives' tale,' scoffed Henry. 'Look, I grow a lot of herbs in pots all year round. Why don't you use those? No-one would know the difference.'

'Mr Witchell,' said Annabel stiffly. 'If I have told you once, I've told you a hundred times. They have to be hand-picked in the wild, often just before dawn with the dew on them and at the proper season.'

'Well then, my dear,' said Henry, 'You have got a problem and I don't know how you are going to get over it.'

'The answer's simple, Mum,' said Betsy. 'You just make remedies when you do have the herbs and any others will just have to wait until the proper time.'

'There, you see,' Annabel glanced at her husband. 'Betsy's right. We can only do what we can do.'

When she delivered the next batch of remedies she explained this to Mr Longbridge who nodded thoughtfully.

'You do what you think is best,' he said.

A few weeks went by and Annabel and Betsy began to settle into a routine of gathering herbs on Barrow Hill, drying them, pounding them in a pestle and mortar and making them up into remedies.

Because of the demands on them Annabel began to get worried about the extra quantities they were picking and thought of looking for other spots but on Barrow Hill she knew all the best spots.

The days went by happily and productively until one day when Annabel was shopping in Mrs Garner's Post Office Stores. The Pettit sisters were also in the shop talking at the counter. As Annabel came in with her basket the conversation stopped. She had the feeling that they were talking about her. Emily Pettit looked particularly embarrassed.

'Good morning, Mrs Witchell,' they both chorused.

'Good morning, ladies,' she replied.

While Annabel was waiting to be served Emily came up to her timidly and said, 'I hope you don't mind me saying so, Mrs Witchell, but the last remedy of yours I bought from Longbridge's shop in Barrow didn't do me any good at all. Have you changed the recipe? The last one I got from you worked fine but not this one.'

'Which one was it?' asked Annabel.

Emily blushed and said, 'It was the one for helping your stomach.'

Rosemary Pettit said bluntly, 'It was the one for helping your digestion so that you don't make so many smells.'

Annabel was quite surprised. 'I haven't changed the recipe for that one in years. It usually works very well,' she said.

This was just the start of it. Over the next few days a number of women told her, some accusingly, that her remedies didn't work any more.

'This is serious,' said Annabel over dinner. 'What is going on? I think we had better pay George Longbridge a visit.'

'It sounds suspicious to me,' said Henry. 'As soon as you let him sell your remedies they stop working.'

They discussed it over the meal and decided that Annabel and Betsy would go over to Barrow Magna and visit the shop. 'Only we won't go when it's open,' said Annabel 'We'll go tonight after closing time. That way we can have a good look round without interference.'

Henry offered to drive them over in the truck but Annabel said 'No, this is a chance for Betsy to take her first long trip on a broomstick. You can take my old one, I'll lead the way and you can follow.'

'But, Mum,' said Betsy turning pale, 'I've only played with your broomstick taking short hops in the garden. Barrow Magna is a long trip. What if anyone sees us?'

'Travelling by broomstick is what witches do, my girl. Anyway there's no moon tonight so we probably won't be seen.'

They left, Annabel leading and Betsy following, shakily at first but as they soared into the night sky gradually gaining confidence until at last she was riding side by side with her mother.

'This is fun,' she said. 'Why didn't you let me do this before?'

'Because you weren't ready, my girl.' Then, as Betsy wobbled a bit to the right, 'Hold on tight and keep your mind on what you are doing.'

Annabel was almost right about not being seen. They sailed over the rooftops of Barrow Magna where all the good folks of the town were sitting safely watching their televisions or preparing for bed. But one person did see them.

Barrow Magna, although only a small town in the Cotswolds, had its share of drunks and one was huddled in the doorway of the gift shop opposite Longbridge's Health Food Shop as they arrived.

The spectacle of two broomsticks landing in perfect formation was too much for Dicky Osborne so he buried his head in his hands and huddled into his tattered overcoat.

Annabel was aware of him as they landed and set a simple spell on him so that he fell into a deep sleep.

'When he wakes up in the morning he won't remember a thing,' she said. 'Come on, let's go into the shop.'

There in the window was the big poster advertising Witchell's remedies. By the time Betsy had dismounted from her broomstick Annabel had examined the lock on the door.

'Piece of cake,' she said and with that the door flew open.

'Better bring the broomsticks inside. Don't want anyone stealing them.'

Broomsticks remain charged with energy for about an hour after flight so they were still hovering in the air at waist height and Betsy was able to steer them easily into the shop.

'We'll use fairy light,' said Annabel. 'That's light we can see by but no-one outside the shop will be able to see it.'

The shop lit up as light as day. Annabel and Betsy stood looking at the rows of shelves.

'There are your bottles over there,' said Betsy pointing to a shelf at the back of the counter.

Annabel peered carefully at the array of bottles and packages. 'They look like mine,' she said 'But I don't remember giving George Longbridge so many. Perhaps he had some left over from the last batch.'

She held up a package of herbs. 'This one isn't mine,' she said. 'It's got my label on but it's for curing insomnia and I didn't make this up. Let's take a look in the back.'

The door to the storeroom at the back wasn't locked and once inside they found themselves in a room filled with boxes and boxes of stock items. Going over to the desk in the corner Annabel was surprised to find a whole stack of blank Witchell remedy labels ready to have the name of the remedy written on them. Meanwhile, Betsy had moved over to the back corner. There she found a supply of empty bottles and what looked like a large water container. On the floor near the container were a number of bottles that had been filled with a pinkish liquid and labelled Witchell's Stomach Mixture. She called Annabel over. 'Look, Mum,' she said pointing. 'George Longbridge has been making up your remedies himself.'

They found that this was exactly what he had been doing.

Obviously Annabel's deliveries hadn't been enough for him so he had not only been making more of the things she had supplied; he had been inventing other remedies.

'The bottles just seem to be coloured water, but he's done a bit better with the packages,' said Annabel opening one, labelled 'a cure for toothache' and sniffing at the contents. This does at least contain Valerian but it wouldn't do anyone much good as a remedy for toothache.'

'What are we going to do?' asked Betsy.

'I'll tell you what you're going to do, my girl. Go and get the broomsticks ready to fly. I'm going to have a think about this and will be with you in a minute.'

Betsy could always tell when Annabel was going to cast a spell as she went rigid and her gaze seemed to look into the future. She went out to the broomsticks.

When the shop was locked up again they both set off, leaving the town drunk still huddled in the opposite doorway.

At home Betsy made a perfect landing and they both went into the house to be greeted by Henry. 'I've just made a fresh cup of tea. I'm sure you would like one. '

Betsy and her mum sat in front of the blazing fire clutching mugs of tea.

'Well, what are we going to do now?' asked Betsy.

'Tomorrow, you and I are going over to Longbridge's shop to see the fun,' said Annabel.

'What fun?' asked Henry innocently.

'Never you mind,' his wife replied. 'Betsy's going to get

a lesson in 'out of the body' experience so we can see old Longbridge without him seeing us.'

'Oh, not that again,' sighed Henry. 'You lying up in the bedroom looking as though you're dead. Must you teach Betsy that one?'

'If she is to become a proper witch she has to learn it all, and now is the best time.' Annabel looked sternly at her husband.

'I have practised a bit,' said Betsy. 'But I haven't got any further than looking down at myself in bed while I float up to the ceiling.'

'Well that's good enough,' said Annabel 'At least you have the technique and tomorrow will be the real thing.'

Tomorrow came and it was time. Early in the morning Annabel gave Betsy her final instructions. Betsy listened attentively although she knew most of it already. They agreed to meet in Betsy's room. Annabel would come and collect her.

Ten minutes later Betsy was hovering rather uncertainly above the bed where her prone figure was stretched out as though she was asleep. Annabel came into the room in spirit form, clasped her gently by the hand and off they floated through the morning air.

'This is better than the broomstick,' thought Betsy.

'When it works properly,' Annabel thought back at her. 'The problem is if something gives you a bit of a jolt you might find yourself snapping back into your body.'

This time everything went well and they circled over Barrow Magna coming down as Mr Longbridge was opening his shop. They just managed to squeeze through the door as he closed it.

'That was silly,' said Annabel. 'In this state we can float through closed doors,' and she demonstrated by floating in and out of the shop.

'However, old habits die hard,' she said. 'Come over here by the wall.'

Betsy nestled up to her like two flies on a windowpane. They had to wait for a while for the first customer to come in.

Meanwhile Mr L was busying himself in the back room.

'I'm going to have a look at what he's doing.' Annabel floated off the wall and circled in behind him.

Talking and even shouting is limited by distance but thought waves as well as only being received by the person they are intended for, have an almost unlimited range.

Betsy received Annabel's thoughts very clearly. 'Mr L is making up some more Witchell remedies. He's got a nerve, but he's going to learn his lesson soon.'

'What have you done, Mum?' asked Betsy.

'Just you wait and see,' said her mother coming back to the wall beside Betsy.

Mr L was just putting the new bottles on the Witchell remedy shelf when the first customer came in.

'Morning, Mr Longbridge. Nice day,' said the woman who obviously knew him.

'Morning, Mrs Cobblett. All the nicer for seeing you. What can I get you today?'

'Another bottle of that stomach mixture if you would. The other one didn't seem to do me much good. Perhaps this one will be better.'

'Of course, Mrs Cobblett. Here we are.' Mr L lifted down one of the bottles he had just prepared.

As he handed it to her it exploded in her face. The cap came off showering both of them with pink liquid.

'Oh!' Mrs Cobblett was beside herself with anger. 'Look at my new coat. Ruined and I've only just bought it.'

Mr L took a cloth from the side and dabbed it ineffectually at the rapidly spreading stain. 'I'm so sorry I don't know how it happened. What can I do to make amends?'

Mrs Cobblett drew herself up to her full height. 'I don't think I want you do anything more,' she said sweeping out of the shop. 'Good day.'

'The spell is working nicely,' said Annabel smiling at Betsy. 'Let's watch one more and then we will go.'

Mr L mopped up the mess as best he could and threw the bottle into the waste bin.

Soon two other customers came in both asking for Witchell remedies. One was lucky as she asked for a genuine remedy but the other one suffered a pink shower from the fake bottle.

'I've seen enough,' Annabel led Betsy out of the shop and soon they were speeding back towards their house. Landing safely in their bodies they met downstairs as Henry came in from the garden.

'Hullo, you two, how did it go?'

'Oh, Pa, it was so funny in the shop but flying out of your body is much better than wobbling about on a silly old broomstick.'

'It's not silly and it's not old,' said Annabel. 'You need to learn both and do whatever suits the occasion. In this case we wanted to see and not be seen.'

Betsy then gave her father a detailed account of what had happened. 'You should have seen them,' she said. 'The fake bottles exploding and showering them with pink froth.'

'I think we shall be getting a visit from Mr L soon,' said Annabel and sure enough they did.

He stood on the doorstep looking bedraggled. It was raining hard at the time. Annabel let him in and he collapsed into a chair. He was almost in tears.

'I don't know what's wrong,' he said between sniffs. 'Every time I sell a bottle of your herbal remedies it explodes over me and the customer. I'm at my wits' end. Can you tell me what to do?'

'Of course I can,' said Annabel. 'But first, stop snivelling and listen to me.'

Mr Longbridge sat up straight like a naughty child and blew his nose loudly.

'I can tell you what's wrong. You have been making your own remedies and selling them under my name.' She held up her hand. 'Don't trouble to deny it, I know.'

'Yes, I have' said Mr L penitently. 'But it was only because so many people wanted them and you don't supply me with enough.'

'That's not good enough,' snapped Annabel. 'You deceived people using my good name to fool them into drinking coloured water.'

Mr L realized that it wasn't a good idea to antagonise a witch so he listened carefully perched on the edge of his chair.

'I won't do it again,' he said. 'I will just sell your genuine remedies in the future.'

'That you won't,' said Annabel 'You will never sell them again.' She fixed him with an eagle eye. 'And, you will return all of mine you have left over and destroy the fake ones for if you don't I shall know and a worse fate will overtake you!'

Mr L shuddered as Annabel indicated that the interview was over. He hurried out of the house, into his car and drove away.

'And that's good riddance to bad rubbish,' said Annabel rubbing her hands together.

Next Saturday Annabel was back at the end of Henry's market stall and her sign said: 'Only genuine Witchell remedies sold here.'

Artist in Residence

'There's no harm in it, Mum,' Betsy protested. 'Tommy is a good artist and he only wants to paint my portrait.'

'As long as that's all he wants to paint, my girl,' Annabel said grimly.

Her idea of sitting for a painting was the old-fashioned notion that the sitter always posed in the nude and got seduced by the artist in the break time.

'It's nothing like that,' insisted Betsy. 'It's just a head and shoulders, that's all.'

'I reckon I ought to come and see this artist of yours to see what's going on,' said Annabel.

About six months ago a caravan had appeared in Bill Baxter's field next to the duck pond, just after the Mr Varley affair, and nosy as always the Pettit sisters had enquired from Mrs Garner at the Post Office Stores about the newcomer.

'You mean Mr Tucker,' said Mrs Garner, always ready to impart information. 'He's an artist you know. Down from London. Wanted quiet surroundings in which to paint. Fed up with the rat race. A nice quiet gentleman.'

'I don't know if I approve of artists,' Rosemary Pettit said. 'You never know what they will get up to.' And soon, because the Pettit sisters knew, the whole village knew and looked on the newcomer with awe.

'It isn't every day you get an artist in your village,' Henry said. 'I wonder if he's famous?'

'Shouldn't think so,' said Annabel. 'Whoever heard of an artist called Tommy Tucker? If you ask me it sounds fishy as though that isn't his real name and now he's gone and asked our Betsy to sit for him.'

'Oh, let me do it, Mum. He's such a nice old gentleman.' Betsy's idea of old was anyone aged thirty or over.

This is what led to Annabel visiting the artist. As she drew near to the field she smiled, remembering the fun they had preventing Mr Varley from building houses on the site. The duck pond was the only thing left after the fairies had helped her by flooding the field.

It was a lovely spot at the base of Barrow Hill. As she approached the large caravan she could see a figure painting at an easel under a sun awning.

'Mr Tucker?' she asked.

'That's me,' said the rather large gentleman laying his

brush carefully down on his palette. 'Whom do I have the pleasure of addressing?'

Annabel looked at the painting. It was a landscape of mountains and trees with a deer in the foreground.

'I'm Betsy's mother,' she said.

'Hmmm,' he said. 'I suppose you have come to tell me not to paint Betsy in the nude?'

Annabel was impressed. 'You must be a mind reader,' she said.

'Not really,' Mr Tucker smiled. 'It's just that everyone thinks that artists have evil designs on their sitters but it's certainly not true in this case. Betsy is a lovely girl and I just wanted to paint her portrait.'

'I'm glad to hear it,' she said. 'In any case this was really only a courtesy call welcoming you to the village.'

'That means a cup of tea,' he said. 'I don't get many visitors except those awful Pettit sisters who came round awhile ago.'

Annabel laughed. 'Don't you mind them,' she said. 'They poke their noses into everything in the village but they mostly don't mean any harm.'

'Come in and have that tea,' he said carefully putting a cloth over the painting.

They went into the caravan. Annabel was surprised to see how neat everything was. In her mind artists were untidy beings living a bohemian life but this one was obviously different. Even his completed paintings were stacked neatly in one corner.

She began to like Tommy Tucker and after a cup of tea with him, liked him even more.

'Mind you,' she said to Henry later. 'That man's got something to hide. I like him but there's a secret there somewhere.'

'Is it all right to sit for my portrait?' asked Betsy.

'Yes, my love. I don't see any harm in him and I would know if there was. See if you can get him talking about himself. There's something bottled up in there and it can't be doing him any good.'

And that was how it was left. Betsy went for her sitting until some days later she burst into the kitchen where Annabel was making an apple pie.

'The picture's finished and here's a pencil sketch he made of me. He's given it to me. Look, look.' She thrust a page from an artist's sketchbook into Annabel's floury hands.

Annabel backed off. 'No, wait until I get the flour off my hands otherwise I will ruin it.' She quickly washed her hands and took the page. It was a careful pencil sketch, a finely drawn head and shoulders. There was no doubt as to the identity of the sitter.

Annabel took it through to the sitting room and Betsy followed.

'Can we frame it, Mum? Maybe Mr Tucker will become famous and then I will be famous as the unknown model.' She gave a little twirl and then sat down heavily on the settee.

Henry had just come in. Annabel handed him the picture.

'It looks pretty good to me,' he said. 'It's just like our beautiful daughter.' Betsy blushed and shook her head.

'He is certainly a good artist but I still get that feeling about him,' said Annabel.

* * *

Next day Annabel took some pains to accidentally meet the Pettit sisters in the Post Office Stores. It wasn't difficult to bring the conversation round to the mysterious Mr Tucker.

'And he is mysterious,' said Rosemary Pettit. 'He sets off once every few weeks in that old car of his with sacks draped over something he is trying to hide in the back.'

'No mystery there,' said Annabel. 'I expect he is just taking his painting to be sold.'

'He certainly comes back next day without them,' said Emily Pettit.

Annabel marvelled at the way the Pettit sisters kept an eye on everything in the village. Bill Baxter had once said that you only needed to sneeze at one end of the village and because of the Pettit sisters everyone would know you had a cold within minutes.

Discussing this with Henry afterwards she said, 'I wonder where he goes to sell his pictures? There's no art gallery nearby that I know of. The nearest is probably in Gloucester.'

'Why don't you follow him and find out, if you are that curious?' said Henry.

'Good idea,' said Annabel. 'I'll do better than that.

I'll track him with the crystal ball then we'll know where he goes.'

'Leave him alone, Mum,' said Betsy. 'He's done you no harm.'

'I'm more than curious for curiosity's sake,' said Annabel. 'I feel he needs help. I'm going to find out why and I will help him if I can.'

Days passed and the village went on as normal. Mr Tucker could be seen outside his caravan under the awning painting with just short trips to the Post Office Stores to buy his food. Annabel made discrete enquiries from Olive Garner.

'He must live mainly out of tins,' Olive told her. 'Although I've got a wine and spirits licence he never orders anything like that. Proper teetotaller he seems to be.'

'Unless he gets it outside the village,' said Rosemary Pettit who was standing by listening.

Eventually Mr Tucker made a move. One morning early he loaded up his car with paintings, putting sacking over them as usual. The village always woke early and as he drove away he was observed not only by the Pettit sisters but also by Annabel.

'Right,' she said. 'After breakfast, I'm going to do a bit of tracking.'

She took herself off to her den and took her crystal ball from the cupboard. Giving it a polish with a duster she set it on a stand in front of her. Locking the door and pulling down the blinds she sat in semidarkness and concentrated.

The best way of describing what she saw was like gazing into a small circular-shaped television screen but because it was a globe of glass the image seemed to float in the middle of the ball.

She got on his track fairly quickly but it soon became obvious that this wasn't a short trip. Annabel raised the blind and unlocked the door, placing a cloth over the crystal.

To pass the time she got on with making up a tincture of marigold for Mrs Cooke to use as a digestive tea for her husband.

At intervals she lifted the cloth and peered into the crystal but Mr Tucker was still chugging off into the distance. It wasn't until sometime after lunch that Annabel saw he had arrived in a city and it soon became apparent that it was London.

Watching closely, she saw the car draw up outside an art gallery called the Charlton Gallery. She moved the scene slightly to the right and was able to see the street sign which read 'Charlton Street. S.W.1'

Moving the scene back to the gallery entrance she saw Mr Tucker go into the shop and come out again with a man in overalls who helped him take the pictures into the shop. After a short while he came out again looking pleased with himself, got into the car and drove off.

Exhausted from the concentration, Annabel took the crystal ball from the stand and put it and the cloth back into the cupboard. Passing Henry on the way back to the house she asked, 'I'm making some tea. Do you want some?'

Henry who was pricking out some seedlings, straightened up.

'Good idea,' he said following her into the house.

Betsy was just back from school and the three of them sat round the kitchen table.

'What happened about Mr Tucker?' she asked eagerly.

'Sells his pictures in London,' Annabel said. 'Nothing wrong with that but I'd like to take a look at them.'

'London's a long way to go to satisfy yourself about a mystery man,' said Henry.

'You're forgetting, my lad,' said Annabel sharply. 'I don't need to go there in person. I'll project myself there in an out-of-the-body session.'

"I'll never get used to you doing that,' said Henry. 'It gives me a fair turn to see you lying flat out on the bed as though you're dead.'

'Better than paying the fare to London and back,' said Annabel. 'I'll go tomorrow.'

The next day about mid afternoon Mr Tucker came back in his old car about the time that Annabel projected herself to London.

The only problem with the out-of-the-body technique is you can't materialise and be seen by other people. However, on this occasion it suited Annabel as she hovered in front of the entrance to the gallery passing in with someone else as they opened the door. This wasn't strictly necessary but she disliked the idea of passing through a brick wall or a plate glass window.

The gallery was laid out in typical fashion. It was basically a wide open space with paintings round the walls. Annabel examined them with interest. Each painting had a small label near it giving the title of the painting, the name of the artist and the price.

Annabel said to Henry afterwards, 'You can't imagine the price of those paintings. Who would pay prices like that?'

'Did you get any information on Mr Tucker,' he asked.

'Not a thing,' she said. 'There were no paintings by Tommy Tucker at all but Betsy's picture was there.'

Betsy clapped her hands, 'Was it Mum?'

'Yes,' said Annabel, 'and the artist's name wasn't Tommy Tucker, it was Jason Tarbury. More than that, I overheard an assistant telling someone that Jason Tarbury, the famous artist, had died six months ago in a car crash.'

'Well, what do you know,' said Henry. 'Wasn't that the time that Tommy Tucker turned up in Happy End?'

'Either Mr Tucker is faking the pictures of a dead artist, or he is this Tarbury fellow and I am going to find out,' said Annabel.

Next day early, the sun was just coming up as Annabel set off to see Tommy Tucker.

The artist was out under his awning having breakfast at a picnic table.

'Mrs Witchell, come and have a cup of tea.' He dived into the caravan and brought out a folding chair for her to sit on.

Annabel sank into it. 'Thank you, Mr Tucker or should

I call you Mr Tarbury?'

He looked at her for a moment and then said, 'Hold on, I'll get a cup for you.'

When he came back he put the cup and saucer on the table and poured her tea.

'No sugar,' Annabel waved the sugar bowl away. 'Well, what's it to be?'

Jason Tarbury put the teapot down carefully.

'Now you've guessed my little secret, what do you intend to do about it?' he asked.

'What would you like me to do?' Annabel countered.

'Let me tell you a story,' he said.

Annabel settled back in the chair and sipped her tea.

'I am, as you guessed, Jason Tarbury,' he said. 'You may not know it but I came to fame three years ago with a painting that people call the Tarbury Venus.

'This was a painting of a nude woman. She was a great friend of mine and I painted her regularly. Her name was Christine and although we weren't married I loved her dearly.

'When we first met I was a struggling artist in London and she was a successful model. We met at an artist's gallery in North London where I had a studio and the moment we set eyes on each other we knew that there was mutual attraction. She became my lover.'

Annabel pursed her lips and tried not to look disapproving but Jason caught the look and said, 'The attraction between us was so strong it was frightening. To cut a long story short, she agreed to sit for me and because of the magnetism between us I painted what is considered to be my masterpiece, the Tarbury Venus. It was an immediate success.

'Fortunately I had secured a regular commitment with a gallery in the West End of London to show my paintings. No sooner was the Tarbury Venus displayed than at least five people wanted to buy it. Gregory, the gallery owner, was delighted and immediately organised an auction, the higher bidder to have the picture.

'To my surprise the bidding went to thousands of pounds and even after the gallery's commission I found myself a moderately wealthy man.

'From then on I could do no wrong. Everyone seemed to want a Tarbury painting. The money flowed in. It was perhaps the happiest time of my life. I was in love with the perfect woman, I had my painting and money kept rolling in.

'What more could I want. By this time Christine had moved into my flat and I thought it was time that we moved into something larger where she would have her own room and I could have a larger studio. Also, I wanted to marry her.

'I had just decided all of this when I went out and bought an engagement ring meaning to propose to her that evening. I know that sounds old-fashioned.'

Annabel shook her head, 'No it doesn't. Go on.'

'Christine had kept her modelling commitments going and was out that day on a photo shoot in Central London. I got back quite late as I had met a fellow artist and had a drink with him in a Park Lane pub. When I arrived back at the flat it was in darkness. I thought Christine was still out. She had her own key.

'I went into the bedroom to change but when I switched on the light, to my horror, Christine was lying on the bed stabbed to the heart. The blood staining the front of her white blouse.'

Jason stopped, eyes full of tears holding out his hands to Annabel.

'There was nothing I could do. I held her in my arms but she was gone. I got blood on my clothes but I didn't notice at the time. I phoned for the police and an ambulance, hoping against hope that I was wrong and that there was a spark of life left but of course there wasn't.

'The police were very polite but I was taken in for questioning. She had been stabbed with the paper knife that she had given me as a present. The window in the bedroom was open and it looked as though whoever had done it had escaped down the fire escape.

'The time of death was set at the time when I had been in the pub and this was collaborated by my artist drinking partner. I was released but I am sure you know all about the finger of suspicion. In that respect a community of artists is like a small village where rumours start and grow.'

Annabel nodded her agreement.

'After that I had to move. In any case I no longer wanted to live there so I went into rented accommodation in another part of London, then I had this idea. If you examine the lives of famous pop stars you find that a number of them died young but their legend lives on. Anything associated with them seems to increase in value. So, I planned my own death. I reasoned that after my death my paintings would acquire a rarity value and should increase in price.

'The easiest thing seemed to be a motor accident. My idea was to have my car slew off the road and explode as it went over a cliff. I've seen it done many times on films but when I came to examine the details it seemed difficult to achieve. In the end I just sent my car over a cliff into the sea below making sure that I jumped clear before it went over.

'When the car was recovered because the car door was open and no body was found it was assumed that the body had been washed out to sea and I was free to start a new life. I needed to adopt a new personality so I decided to take the gallery owner, a good friend of mine, into my confidence. You can imagine Gregory's surprise when, a week after my 'death' I walked into the gallery. I explained my plan to him and he agreed. I would disappear into the country painting Jason Tarbury masterpieces for him to sell and we would split the proceeds.

'Up until now it has worked perfectly. I am very happy in your lovely village and want to continue living here.'

He looked appealingly at Annabel, 'Now that you have found me out, what do we do?'

Annabel sat and thought for a long moment then she looked straight at him.

'We do absolutely nothing,' she said. 'But how did you fake your new identity? These days you need a birth certificate, passport and evidence that you are who you say you are even to open a bank account.'

He smiled at her. 'That's easy,' he said. 'You see, I thought I could never be a famous artist with a name like Tommy Tucker so I became Jason Tarbury but my real name is Tommy Tucker. I think my mother had a sense of humour as she told me that I always wanted my supper so she called me Tommy.'

Annabel smiled and said, 'Well Tommy Tucker I think it is time you put Jason Tarbury behind you and began to live your own life. Build a reputation in your own name.'

A weight seemed to fall from his shoulders. He gave Annabel a hug and waved as she crossed the field.

'Anything I can do to help you,' he called. 'Let me know.'

6

Beauty and the Beast

The Reverend Alistair Harding looked contentedly out of the vestry door. Billie the goat was happily munching away at the grass between the gravestones. For once Bill Baxter, the poacher who owned the field at the foot of Barrow Hill, had been of some help to the church.

Desperate to find someone to mow the grass in the churchyard, the Reverend Harding had put an advertisement in the Parish magazine appealing for help. As usual no-one had volunteered until Bill Baxter had offered to lend his goat.

'He makes a fine lawnmower, Reverend,' he said. 'He's forever eating grass and sometimes I find it hard to find enough for him. Well-fertilized grass in the churchyard will do him good.'

So Billie became the volunteer grass cropper for the church.

Talking to his wife Isabel over breakfast next morning, Alistair confessed his misgivings about giving a goat free access to the churchyard.

'I thought you tethered a goat,' he said. 'But Mr Baxter said to let him roam free and it seems to be working.'

And so it did until someone left the church gate open.

Billie tired of eating grass escaped from the churchyard and made his way down the village. The Pettit sisters found out about it next morning when Emily's shrieks brought Rosemary to the window.

'Look,' she cried. 'There's a goat in the garden and it's eating our flowers.'

Indeed, Billie had already munched his way through a succulent border of marigolds and was starting on the sweet peas.

Bolder than her sister, Rosemary ran outside into the garden.

'Go away,' she cried, making flapping movements with her hands. Billie looked up with an interested eye and went on munching.

Everyone in the village knew that the goat had been press ganged into church lawn mowing service so Rosemary ran back into the house and rang the vicar.

Reverend Harding was eating his way through a bowl of cornflakes when the phone rang. His wife handed him the phone and whispered, 'It's the Pettit sisters, something about the goat.'

Alistair had to listen to the distraught voice of

Rosemary Pettit punctuated with shrieks from Emily in the background. Putting on his most pacifying voice he assured her that he would get in touch with Mr Baxter and get the goat towed away.

Unfortunately, good man that he was, he tried to contact Bill Baxter but was told that he wasn't available. What Bill's wife didn't tell him was that her better (or worse) half was still in bed with a colossal hangover caused by overindulgence at the Fox's Revenge the night before.

This left Alistair with a problem. He could go to the Pettit's house and haul the beast off himself, but vicars do not handle goats, he thought. So who could he turn to for help?

At that moment he must have felt that divine providence had taken a hand as he heard a ring at the doorbell and who should be at the door but Betsy Witchell, Annabel's daughter.

His wife led her into the sitting room and offered her a cup of tea. Meanwhile Alistair had made up his mind to ask Betsy if her father Henry would help. He hurried into the sitting room to greet Betsy and put the problem to her.

'Good morning, Betsy. What can I do for you this bright and sunny morning?' he asked, holding his own problem in check for a moment.

To his surprise Betsy turned a bright shade of pink and, turning her head away from him, said in a small strangled voice, 'It's the beauty contest in Barrow Magna next week. I need someone to sponsor my entry and Pa thought you might sign the form for me.' She turned and looked at him.

'Beauty contest? I see. Prettiest girl in the neighbourhood sort of thing?' He nodded thoughtfully.

Now that she had said it, Betsy's words tumbled out in a rush.

'And that Lucy Baxter is entering and everyone says I'm better looking than she is. Will you sign for me, Vicar?' She looked at him hopefully.

His own troubles forgotten for the moment, he said, 'Of course, my dear.'

Betsy produced a crumpled piece of paper from the pocket of her dress.

'Let me find a pen.' He rummaged around in the top drawer of his desk. 'Why is it whenever you want a pen you can never find one?'

His wife, who had been listening to this, came forward with a pen in her hand. 'Is this what you're looking for, dear?' she said patiently.

He took the pen, looked briefly at the form and signed it at the bottom with a flourish.

'There, my dear, and may I wish you every good luck in the competition.'

Should I be encouraging a young girl to parade in a bathing costume in front of a lot of other people, he thought. He knew he was old-fashioned but he justified it by saying to himself that young folk today are more forward than they were in his day.

As Betsy got up to go, carefully folding the entry form and putting it back in her pocket he said hurriedly, 'There is another matter that I would like your father's help on rather urgently.'

Betsy turned back towards him. 'Anything Pa can do to help, I'm sure he will,' she said.

'Well, this concerns a goat,' he began.

'You mean old Bill Baxter's goat,' she laughed. 'I saw him down at the Pettit's eating their flowers as I went by. I nearly went in and dragged him out but he can be awful mean if he's a mind to, so I left him at it.'

'That's just it,' said Alistair. 'I can't get Mr Baxter to come for him and I promised Miss Pettit I would do something about it. Is your father any good with goats?'

Betsy smiled. 'I don't think Pa could handle him, not when Billie's enjoying himself so much, but I'm sure Mum could help. She has a way with animals.'

Alistair breathed a sigh of relief. 'If you're going back home now, would you ask her? It's fairly urgent as if we don't stop him their garden will be destroyed.'

'I'll go back straight away,' Betsy made for the door.

'Thank you for signing my form, Reverend. I'll tell Mum about the goat. She will help I'm sure.'

As soon as Annabel heard about the goat, she stopped what she was doing, put on her coat and went round to the Pettit's house.

Emily looked out of the window to see Annabel taking hold of Billie's collar and leading him towards the gate. Both of them went to the door to thank her.

'We were so worried,' explained Rosemary. 'You see, if

the goat had reached the chrysanthemums it would have ruined our chances in the flower show next week.'

'Let me lead Billie out and then I'd like to look at your chrysanths,' she said.

She led Billie to the gate and whispered in his ear. Billie gave her a sideways look and then set off obediently down the village.

'That should do it,' she said. 'He ought to find his way home now.'

They watched as the goat trotted off down the road.

'Right,' said Annabel. 'Now let's look at these prize chrysanths of yours.'

Emily led the way down the garden to the greenhouse where patch of almost open golden chrysanthemums were sunning themselves.

'We don't win of course,' said Emily. 'But we always try.'

Annabel surveyed the nodding flower heads.

'I don't know why not,' she said. 'These look really good to me.'

Rosemary glanced at her sister and said, 'The problem is Mr Tomlinson from Barrow Magna. He always enters his chrysanthemums and he always wins. His look perfect for the judging but ours seem to wilt overnight. I don't know how he does it but he must cheat in some way.'

'Now you don't know that, sister dear,' said Emily.

'He does, I'm sure of it,' Rosemary looked at Annabel who was admiring the flowers.

'You might win this year,' she said dreamily. 'These are

really good.'

She said goodbye and the Pettit sisters went back into the house.

Meanwhile Billie was trotting happily back to his field when he was distracted by Olive Garner at the Post Office Stores. She was putting out some trays of vegetables. Billie caught the smell of fresh cauliflower and it was too much for him to bear. He headed towards them.

Olive didn't particularly mind goats although she thought of them as nasty smelly creatures but when they threatened her cauliflowers she became like a mother hen with her chicks.

'Shoo, you smelly beast.' She flapped her apron.

Billie transferred his attention from the vegetables to Olive. He took half a step towards her and then backed away across the road where there was a wide area of beaten earth known locally as 'the drive'. He stood waiting for her to go back in the shop. She shook her fist and went back into the shop.

Young Chris Garner, Olive's son, was playing happily at the entrance to the drive on his scooter. Chris' scooter was in his imagination a powerful car and putting his foot down on the accelerator pedal he swung his scooter into the road and prepared to cross back to his mother's shop where he knew he would be rewarded with a sweet.

What he didn't see was Jackson's Bakery van coming up the hill from Malmesbury. Les Barnes a young lad who had only just passed his driving test was driving the van.

He found the gears on the old van a bit of a trial especially going up hills.

He reached the brink of the hill just as Chris started to cross the road. Les' attention was on his gear change and he failed to see the small figure scoot in front of him.

Disaster would have stuck if Billie the goat hadn't struck first. Fortunately for everyone Billie decided to cross the road at exactly the same moment to have another go at Olive's cauliflowers but Chris' scooter was in his way.

The van was within an inch or so of Chris when Billie did the thing that goats always do when faced with an obstacle. Head down, he butted Chris and his scooter hard, shooting him forward out of the path of the van. Billie wasn't as fortunate, for as Chris and his scooter shot forward the van struck Billie and ran over one of his legs before jerking to a halt.

The squeal of brakes and the animal scream from Billie brought Olive from the shop and Annabel from the Garden Centre opposite. Olive clutched Chris to her while Annabel ran to Billie as Les Barnes jumped out of the van.

Goats are heavy so Annabel called her husband Henry and together he and Les carried the goat over to the Garden Centre.

'I saw it all,' said Olive. 'Fair gave me a turn, but the goat saved Chris's life it did.' She put her arm round Chris who was quite happily eating the sweet she had given him.

Annabel put a herbal poultice on the goat's leg and secured it with a neat splint.

'You won't be trotting around for a while,' she said. 'Perhaps that's just as well. At least Pettit's chrysanths are safe and they might win a prize this time round.'

As though listening to Annabel, Billie rolled over on his side and got to his feet staggering like a young foal. He managed to stand on three legs holding the fourth off the ground when Bill Baxter arrived.

'What have you done to my goat?' he cried.

Annabel sat him down with a cup of tea while she explained.

'Your goat is a hero,' she told him. 'He saved young Chris' life and the injury he got will soon heal so no harm done.'

Bill Baxter was inclined to grumble and said he wanted to claim compensation from Bob Jackson the baker.

Les Barnes was driving but I don't think it was his fault,' said Annabel. 'It all happened so quickly but it was a mercy that Billie was there and butted Chris out of the way.'

'That worked out well,' Annabel said to Henry afterwards. 'Next week's flower show and beauty contest should be interesting with Betsy competing against Lucy Baxter and the Pettit's competing against Mr Tomlinson's chrysanthemums. I wonder what will happen.'

Henry looked at her thoughtfully.

'You're not planning anything, are you?' he asked.

Annabel sat back in her chair smiling.

7

Barrow Magna's Flower Show and Beauty Contest

'**N**o magic,' Annabel said firmly. 'If you are going in for this beauty contest you must win it on your own merits.'

'Yes, Mum,' Betsy said obediently. 'Does that mean you won't be using any spells to help the Pettit sisters with their chrysanthemums?'

'That's a different matter,' said Annabel. 'Maybe I will, and maybe I won't.'

Betsy as we know had already asked the Reverend Harding to sponsor her for the beauty contest where she thought her main rival would be Lucy Baxter. The chrysanthemum episode with Billie the goat had alerted Annabel to the possibility of dirty dealings in the flower show and she was determined that it would be a fair competition for prizes.

The whole village teemed with activity a few days before the event. Fred Todd carefully tended his prize marrow, John Sparrow pulled one carrot out of the ground to see how big it was and if it was growing straight, the Pettit sisters fussed over their flowers.

Emily kept visiting the chrysanthemums and talking to them.

'I know it's silly,' she said. 'But I get the feeling that if I keep telling them they will win then perhaps we shall have more luck over Mr Tomlinson's flowers.'

Henry, Annabel's husband, was of course, involved in the show, as he was responsible for the ornamental shrubs and flowers round the judging platform for the beauty contest. He was also a judge for the vegetable competitions. Annabel had been invited to join a panel of judges for the flower arrangements.

So it was that Henry and Annabel were over at the showground in Barrow Magna on the afternoon before the show. Most of the competitors were also there setting out and arranging their exhibits.

'What security arrangements do they have?' asked Annabel.

Henry scratched his head. 'I don't really know. Why do you ask?'

'The Pettit sisters told me that last year their chrysanths had wilted badly overnight leaving Mr Tomlinson to win the gold medal. It occurred to me that there might be some skulduggery going on.'

The main tent was full of the bustle of people bringing plants in, setting them down and arranging them. There is something in being in a big tent that is very satisfying, the smell of the canvas, and an awareness of being in a lofty space away from the real world. Annabel could feel it but being a witch she also had a feeling of foreboding knowing the temptations that some people might feel if they had set their hearts on winning.

Henry wandered off to talk to someone but when he came back he said, 'I found out about security. Apparently some people stay with their exhibits all night to make sure they aren't interfered with. I was talking to Mr Hoskins who is on the show committee and he said that last year some people complained about plants and vegetables being sabotaged.'

'In that case I think I had better come back tonight myself,' said Annabel.

Witches can do without sleep for long periods if they have to so it was no hardship for Annabel to steal quietly out of the house that night and take a short broomstick ride to the great tent set out on the recreation field at Barrow Magna. She parked her broomstick behind a large sweet chestnut tree at the end of the ground and walked up to the tent.

The tent flaps were down but she could see ghostly lights moving, silhouetting shadows against the canvas walls.

In a moment she was inside. She saw six people equipped with torches patrolling up and down the gangways.

'Hello, Mrs Witchell, come to join us?' said a familiar voice.

'Oh, hello, Fred, I didn't recognise you in the dark.'

Fred Todd loomed out of the darkness.

'We are a sort of vigilante group,' he said. 'Protecting the exhibits and all that.'

Annabel recognised several other figures as they came up to her.

'We are taking it in turns to patrol various parts of the tent,' said Fred. 'Mr Tomlinson here has volunteered to look after the flowers, Mrs Wilkinson the vegetables and so on. Where would you like to go?'

'I think I'll just freewheel for a bit, Fred, if that's all right by you.'

Privately Annabel thought it probably wasn't a good idea for Mr Tomlinson to patrol the flowers section since his chrysanthemums and the Pettit's were in that section.

She could see that the self-appointed guards were doing a good job and that anyone trying any funny business would have a hard time of it. However, Mr Tomlinson was on his own down in the flower section so she decided to go and see how he was getting on.

Moving quietly she saw him take a small bottle from his pocket. 'Going to fertilise your chrysanths?' she said in a loud voice.

Mr Tomlinson jumped, shone his torch on Annabel and hastily crammed the bottle back in his pocket.

'No …yes,' he said. 'Got to keep them fresh for the morning.'

Annabel fixed him with a stare that he couldn't look away from. The torch stayed fixed on Annabel's face.

'Your chrysanths are over there,' she said. 'These are the Pettit's exhibit. I expect you got confused in the dark. Take the torch and go and freshen up your flowers.'

Mr Tomlinson found his feet taking him over to his own exhibit, his hand felt in his pocket and took the bottle out and removed the stopper.

'But …' he said.

'No buts,' said Annabel. 'Now sprinkle it over your flowers. I'm sure it will do them good.'

Mr Tomlinson did as he was told and then stood waiting for further orders.

'Now off you go home,' she said. 'Tell the others you have got to get home and can they cover for you.'

Mr T went like a lamb and she heard him explaining that he had promised his wife he would be back before midnight.

Fred Todd was furious. 'Saying he would come and patrol and then going off like that.'

'I must be going too,' said Annabel. 'I can see you have this all organised, Fred. I'll see you in the morning.'

'Goodnight, Mrs Witchell. I don't think there will be any trouble tonight but you never know.'

'Indeed you don't,' said Annabel smiling. 'Goodnight.'

Before she left she cast a spell over the tent. There won't be any more trouble tonight, she thought. She picked up her broomstick, set off home and before long was snuggled down in her own bed fast asleep.

Next day dawned bright and sunny.

'Thank goodness it's a nice day,' she said to Henry over breakfast. 'What's Betsy up to? She should have been down by now.'

They heard a howl of anguish and Betsy came down the stairs clad only in her bathing costume.

'This stupid thing,' she said wrestling with the elasticated top.

'Here, let me,' Annabel untwisted it. 'Is this what you are going to wear in the contest?'

'It's a bit daring isn't it?' said Henry.

'Oh, Pa, you're so old-fashioned. This isn't half as daring as some of the girls will be wearing.'

Henry turned to Annabel.

'Don't look at me, Henry Witchell. Betsy chose it for herself and it's perfectly respectable in today's terms.'

Henry retreated behind his buttered toast.

'How about some breakfast, young lady?' said Annabel.

'No time for that,' said Betsy. 'I've got to finish getting ready.'

'We had better finish up and get going ourselves,' said Annabel. 'Judges have to be there early.'

She drove with Henry to the ground where the judges were gathering to award the prizes before the public were allowed in. The next hour was taken up with much discussion between the judges, but at last the prizes were awarded.

At ten o'clock everyone crowded in. Cries of delight and disappointment echoed through the tent as the exhibitors saw how their exhibits had been judged.

Emily Pettit came over to Annabel. She could hardly speak.

'We've done it,' she said. 'A gold medal at last. Poor Mr Tomlinson's flowers wilted overnight. Who would have thought it?'

Who indeed, thought Annabel, but out loud she said, 'Congratulations. You deserve it especially since you nearly lost them to the goat.'

Other members of the village were busy congratulating each other, including Fred Todd who had won a gold medal for his marrow. All in all it was a great success for Happy End as they had been awarded quite a number of prizes and there was always healthy rivalry between the village and the town.

Later in the morning everyone gathered round the platform at the end of the tent for the beauty contest.

Betsy was one of seven contestants, the others were Lucy Baxter, four girls from Barrow Magna and a mystery entry. The panel of three judges were from out of town. One was from the local TV station, another was a dress designer from London and the third was rumoured to be a famous film star although no-one seemed to know her name.

The girls, dressed in bathing costumes, had first to parade in front of the judges and then to come forward individually and answer a series of questions about themselves.

Annabel and Henry were so proud of Betsy and they and other people from Happy End applauded like mad when she came on. Lucy Baxter got some applause but it was a bit muted. Of course, the girls from Barrow Magna got lots of applause but when the last girl came on, the mystery entry, there was shocked silence.

'She's absolutely beautiful,' Henry whispered to Annabel, as indeed she was. She behaved and looked like a top model from London. They found out afterwards that she was. The dress designer on the panel had brought one of his girls over for fun telling the other judges about it so that there was no question of her winning the contest.

The judging took some time but the winner was Lucy Baxter.

Betsy was furious.

'That Lucy,' she said. 'She was making eyes at the judges all the time. The rest of us didn't stand a chance. I wish they had given it to Cecilia. She was the London model.'

'You can't win them all, my girl,' said Annabel. 'At least the Pettits got their prize and you did very well even though you didn't win.'

Afterwards when Betsy had gone up to bed she said to Henry, 'Our little girl is growing up, Henry. She will soon be leaving school and going out in the wide world.'

Yes, she's got a lot to learn,' said Henry. 'She is going to have to suffer disappointments but she's a good girl and she is working hard to get to university next year. That's a lot more than Lucy Baxter will ever accomplish stuck behind the bar at the Fox's Revenge.'

And with that they went to bed. The flower show safely over for another year.

8

Sanctuary

The morning of the bric-a-brac sale dawned.

On the previous evening Annabel, Henry and Betsy had put together a selection of plants to go on the plant stall. Annabel had found a few things to go on the bits-and-pieces stall, several old cushions, and a selection of Henry's old gardening tools. She had also persuaded him to part with some of his old vinyl records.

'Goodness knows how valuable these records really are,' said Henry turning them over. 'Look here's one by Al Bowlly. He was called 'England's Bing Crosby'. Do you remember him?'

'Something about him getting killed in the blitz in 1941,' Annabel said. 'I remember you playing that record over and over. 'Love is the sweetest thing' wasn't it?'

'Yes, and here's another 'The very thought of you.'

'I don't know how you can bear to part with them,' said Annabel.

'Well, different times, different places,' said Henry. 'Anyway they are pretty worn out now. Someone else might get some pleasure out of them.'

Later that evening Annabel was just going to bed when the strains of 'Love is the sweetest thing' floated up to her. She went to the top of the stairs and looked down. There was Henry sitting back in his chair listening to Al Bowlly. She smiled and went back into the bedroom.

Once every two years the vicar organised a bric-a-brac sale in aid of the church funds. His idea was that every so often you should clear unwanted junk from your house on the assumption that your junk would be someone else's treasure. It hurt no one and fostered a community spirit. He argued that it was good to give and this was a way of swelling the church funds, which went mainly to the upkeep of the church roof.

This year, he had decided to hold it in the church itself rather than having it in the church hall as before. The old-fashioned pews had long since been removed and replaced by lightweight chairs and kneelers that could easily be lifted out of the way and stacked, allowing the whole floor to be used for the various stalls.

Annabel, Henry, Betsy and many others from the village had volunteered to help clear the chairs and set up the tables before the sale opened at 10.30am.

After an early breakfast, they loaded the truck up and

set off for the church. Apart from the vicar, they were the first to arrive.

Alistair Harding was just putting the key in the big church door.

'I stacked most of the chairs before I locked up at sunset last night,' he said. 'That gives us a bit of a start this morning.'

They went in and made their way towards the tabletops and trestles that had been stacked against the transept wall.

As the vicar had said, most of the chairs had been stacked out of the way but some had been put on the left hand side.

'So that we can have a tea and coffee area,' he explained.

The church seemed strangely empty without the chairs lined up facing the altar. Annabel wandered down what was usually the aisle towards the front of the church. It was still quite dark, as they hadn't yet put the overhead lights on.

To her surprise, there was a dark bundle in front of the altar steps. As she approached, it turned itself into the figure of a man.

'Sanctuary, sanctuary,' cried a feeble voice.

'Vicar, come quickly,' Annabel turned just as the overhead lights came on.

There huddled on the floor was Colonel Blackley from the Manor. Usually an impressive figure fully in control of himself and everyone else he now looked a pathetic figure kneeling as he was on the stone floor and looking pathetically up at her.

'What's the matter Colonel?' asked the vicar arriving at the scene.

'Sanctuary, sanctuary,' was all they could hear.

'Let's get him into the vestry before anyone else comes in,' suggested Annabel. 'Henry, come and help.'

Together Henry and the vicar lifted the Colonel into the vestry where he sat looking like a stranded whale. His head fell forward and he began to snore.

'Best leave him here to recover,' said Annabel. 'I'll get the doctor to take a look at him then we had better get him back to the Manor.'

'Funny though,' said Henry. 'Come to think of it we haven't seen him around much these last few months. I wonder if he has been ill.'

'He's got that couple to look after him, cook and housekeeper, butler and everything else,' said the vicar. 'But you are right, He used to be in church regularly every week but he hasn't been for the last three months to my knowledge.'

'That woman at the Manor is a flighty piece,' said Annabel. 'I wouldn't trust the pair of them an inch. I wonder what has been going on.'

Henry said he would call Dr Everett. Betsy volunteered to sit with the Colonel until the doctor came and so Annabel put him out of her mind, as there was so much to do before people arrived. Stallholders were now coming in and arranging their wares. The vicar had arranged tables for various categories and had volunteers to look after each one.

There were bits and pieces stalls, photographic stalls, cake stalls, clothing stalls, children's stalls, plant stalls, second hand bookstalls (two of these) and a stall selling old records and tapes.

Annabel had offered to help with the tea and cakes in the special roped off area in the west wing of the church.

Ten o'clock came and already there was a queue outside the church door waiting patiently to get in, huddled under umbrellas, coats drawn up against the drizzly rain.

'We must let them in early,' said the Reverend Harding 'The poor things will get terribly wet.'

Although not everything was ready, they opened the door.

The problem with the arrangements became obvious very quickly as people filtered into the church and began to clog the isles between the tables. When planning the layout, the vicar had not left enough space for people to circulate freely.

Fortunately this didn't seem to matter as people crowded in, cheerfully paying fifty pence for admission and the chance to have their ticket drawn in a raffle.

As the morning wore on people escaped from the church with their purchases only to be replaced by other people. Annabel was kept busy serving tea, coffee, cakes and biscuits but was alarmed when Henry came up to her with his arms full of purchases.

'What have you got there, Henry?' she asked.

'I couldn't resist these books,' he said putting them down on a table. 'And there was this set of CD's 'Masters of

Classical Music. I only paid a pound for them and look at this.' He triumphantly flourished a cardboard box. 'A glass chess set and board. Only a pound again.'

'You don't play chess. What good is that?' protested Annabel.

'Thought it might make a nice table decoration and in any case we could learn to play – something to do in the long winter evenings.'

'You're incorrigible, Henry,' Annabel laughed. 'Don't you go buying anything else, especially books. We have too many in the house as it is. In any case, you ought to go and relieve Betsy in the vestry. Has Doctor Everett been to see the Colonel yet?'

'I don't know, but I will find out.' Leaving his purchases with Annabel, Henry pushed and shoved his way through the throng of people to get to the vestry door. As he did so, there was a sudden lull in the noise and two figures dressed in black came through the church door like vultures about to pounce on their prey.

Annabel paused in pouring a cup of tea for Rosemary Pettit.

'Bert Scoggins and his ladyfriend Freda Wilkins,' she said to Rosemary.

'Up to no good, I'll be bound,' said Rosemary. 'I wonder what they are doing here.'

Annabel's first thought was that they were probably looking for the Colonel and she should go over and tell them that he was in the vestry. Fortunately, her second sight kicked in and she knew that they were after the Colonel and that they must protect him from them at all costs. She went to call Henry but he was already way down the church and just about to enter the vestry.

Henry had seen the two ominous figures and without the benefit of Annabel's second sight had come to the same conclusions. He entered the vestry and shut the door firmly. Inside the Colonel was still sprawled in a chair with Betsy sitting anxiously beside him.

'Did the doctor come?' he asked.

'Not yet,' said Betsy. 'He looks awful bad. What shall we do?'

'First thing is to get him away from here,' said Henry. 'I don't know what's going on, but there's those two from the Manor outside in the church looking like Death itself. We don't want them to find him until we know more about it.'

'Let's get him out of the back door and into your truck,' she said. 'Drive him to our place. He will be safe there.'

'Right,' said Henry and together they managed to get him through the door half dragging him down the path until they came to where Henry had parked the truck. Shovelling him into the passenger seat as best they could Henry reversed and drove off.

Betsy went back into the church through the main door to report to Annabel. She saw the pair of them talking to the vicar and knew from the way he was waving his arms about that he was telling them that the Colonel was in the vestry.

'Mum,' Betsy called desperately but Annabel was already looking down the church and had seen what was happening.

Arriving at Annabel's side Betsy said breathlessly, 'We got him away, Mum. Pa's driven him to our house.'

'Good,' Annabel said. 'I don't like the look of this. We need to get to the bottom of it.'

Meanwhile the vicar had disappeared into the vestry with the other two. Annabel thought she could hear raised voices even above the general level of noise.

The vestry door opened and the terrible pair stormed out closely followed by a worried looking vicar who made his way as rapidly as he could to where Annabel and Betsy were standing.

'They told me the Colonel was terribly ill and they were looking after him,' he said. 'The poor man appears to be wandering in his mind. They were very angry to find that he had gone.'

'I suggested that they contact the police but they said they wanted to avoid a fuss. They needed to find him to look after him. Oh dear, oh dear, what with this and the bric-a-brac sale, what a day.'

Betsy expected him to say 'Oh my fur and whiskers' like the white rabbit in Alice in Wonderland, he looked so worried.

'Don't fret, Vicar,' said Annabel. 'Everything is going well. Look around you, people are enjoying themselves. As to the Colonel and those two, just leave them to me.'

She turned to Betsy. 'Off home with you now and I will

be along presently.'

Betsy set off on the short journey back home to tell her father what was happening.

Anyone observing Annabel closely would have noticed a far off look in her eyes as she projected herself into the mind of Bert Scoggins.

'So that's the game is it my lad. Well, we see about that.'

They had promised the vicar that they would help tidy up after the sale, getting the church ready for the Sunday service. Henry came back and as soon as people had left, Annabel and Henry with the other volunteers soon had the church back to normal.

'The stuff that's left over can go to the charity shop in Barrow Magna,' said the vicar.

'I don't know what's wrong with the Colonel,' Henry said as they left the church.

'I do,' said Annabel. 'Scoggins and Freda are up to something very nasty.'

They arrived home to find Betsy giving the Colonel a cup of tea.

'Thank you, my dear,' he said sitting up and looking a little more like his normal self but still obviously weak.

He looked appealingly at Annabel.

'Don't let those devils get me,' he said, devouring a biscuit as though he hadn't eaten for a week.

'Do you want to talk about it?' said Annabel. 'What happened?'

'You may well ask,' he said. 'Scoggins and his girlfriend

have been with me now for about three and a half months and in the beginning they behaved exactly as they should. I never liked either of them much but you know how it is, they came highly recommended from an agency in Cirencester so how was I to know?'

'Know what?' asked Henry.

'Know that they were going to take me over,' he said. 'I trusted both of them. They worked very well at first. He was a model butler and drove me around whenever I wanted him to. She was a reasonable cook and looked after the house, but after a couple of weeks, things began to change.

'I started to feel ill. Nothing very definite, just out of sorts at first. By the time I realised that Frieda was poisoning me it was too late. I realised it almost by accident. By this time, I was so weak that I spent most of my time in bed. You must have noticed that I wasn't around as much as usual?'

'Yes we did,' said Henry. 'We thought nothing of it as you are often away, sometimes for quite long periods.'

'Frieda brought up my soup for lunch and I suppose by that time she was quite sure of herself, and had grown careless. As she opened the door of the room, I saw her drop something into the soup from a small green bottle.

'When she left I tipped the whole thing down the bathroom toilet and flushed it. It took me some effort to get out of bed I can tell you, and then I sat on the bed thinking about the past few weeks.

'At first I had thought it was old age catching up with me.

Frieda and Bert were very nice to me and Bert even offered to go to Barrow Magna to cash a cheque so that I could pay their wages. This became a regular thing. They were doing everything for me and I could hardly stand.

'Yesterday I realised what was happening. After I saw Frieda put something in my soup I decided I must get away from them. In the afternoon when I knew they would be taking a break, I got up, dressed and managed to get out of the house. I wanted to go down to the village but knew I couldn't make it so I headed for the church to contact the vicar.

'Anyone one seeing me would have thought I was drunk. When I arrived at the church I was surprised to find half the chairs missing and sound of someone in the vestry. I am afraid I hid and must have fallen asleep for the next thing I knew it was getting dark and I was locked in. Then I remembered that churches were used as sanctuaries in the old days and so although hungry, I knew I was safe.

'That's the last thing I remember until I opened my eyes and it was morning with the vicar and Annabel standing in front of me.' He leant back in the chair.

Annabel looked concerned. 'The first thing to do is get some nourishing food inside you then we must work out what to do.'

They gave the Colonel the spare room to sleep in and by next day, he was still weak but considerably improved.

Annabel had discussed a plan with Henry and after breakfast set off to the Manor to carry it out.

When she arrived at the Manor Bert Scroggins greeted her at the door and led her into the sitting room where Frieda was lounging on the settee reading the paper. They behaved as though they owned the place.

'Do you have any news of the Colonel?' asked Annabel.

Frieda put down the paper and said in a very false voice. 'We are so worried about him. He is quite ill you know.'

Bert sat beside her. 'We thought he might have been seen in the village or at the sale in the church but we searched everywhere and no sign of him. We are so worried as we are extremely fond of him.'

'Liars,' said Annabel. 'We know exactly what you have been up to and now you are going to pay for it.'

Bert Scroggins made as if to rise but a surprised look came over his face when he found he couldn't move.

'Just a little restraining spell,' said Annabel. 'While I give you a piece of my mind.'

Annabel gave everyone the impression that she was a mild mannered lovely woman but to Bert and Frieda she appeared to be an avenging angel so great was her wrath.

They sat there shattered, unable to move.

'Now we come to the best part,' said Annabel. 'You are both going to go away from here and are never to come back.'

'Just how are you going to do that,' Bert said, with an attempt at bravado.

'Like this,' she said and held them both with a piercing stare. Both Bert and Frieda felt as though she was looking into their innermost souls and that was the last thing they remembered for quite a while.

*   *   *

Henry returned from dropping them at Kemble station reporting that they had caught the train to London safely.

'They will make their way to Edinburgh from there and won't remember a thing about their past lives,' said Annabel.

'Isn't doing that as bad as what they tried to do to the Colonel,' asked Betsy.

'No,' said Annabel. 'They were trying to kill the Colonel. When they get to Edinburgh they will be convinced that it was their idea to go and start a new life in Scotland.'

'Good riddance to bad rubbish,' said the Colonel who was feeling much better after Annabel's ministrations.

'Now I must go and set my house in order but I shall be much more careful who I employ next time. Thanks to you I'm my own man again.'

9

Closing the School

'They can't close the school,' said Annabel.

'Oh yes they can,' said her husband. 'They can do anything they like.'

Betsy looked at him 'Who are 'they?'' she asked.

The family was sitting cosily round the fire one winter's night, having just heard the news from Miss Tatt, headmistress of the village school. She had arrived, very distressed, to ask Henry as unofficial mayor of the village if there was anything he could do about it.

'Who are 'they?' Betsy repeated.

'I don't really know,' replied Miss Tatt, sitting on the settee, looking the faded, washed out old spinster that she was.

'Well I do,' said Henry. 'I'll tell you who is behind this, it's that Counsellor Griffiths, him whose been such a trouble to the Vicar and who has been throwing his weight about in the village. He's got this bee in his bonnet that our children should be bussed over to the school in Cirencester so that they can get what he calls 'a proper education'. Miss Tatt here has been educating us and our children for many a year and it has been good enough for us all up to now.'

'I don't know what the world is coming to,' Annabel patted Miss Tatt on the shoulder. 'How about a nice cup of tea, my love.'

Miss Tatt looked at her gratefully.

'Won't be a minute,' Annabel slipped into the kitchen. 'Don't you go talking about it until I get back,' she said.

Henry warmed his hands in front of the fire while he gave the matter some thought.

By the time Annabel came back with the tea tray he had made up his mind.

'We re going to fight it,' he said. 'The question is how.'

Annabel looked across at Betsy. 'We know how, don't we, love?'

Miss Tatt looked nervously at her as she accepted a steaming cup of tea. 'I don't think I would want you to do anything drastic,' she said.

'Oh, it won't be drastic,' Annabel smiled at her 'Just, well, a bit unusual that's all. Finish your tea Miss Tatt. Then you go home and have a nice rest.' Annabel spoke in her reassuring voice.

'I can't rest while this is going on,' Miss Tatt sobbed.

Both Annabel and Betsy put their arm around her and led her to the door.

'Thank you Annabel,' she said. 'I'll try not to worry now you are going to help me.'

'Wish I could say the same,' Annabel murmured, but out loud she said, 'Don't worry, we'll sort this out for you.'

When they were alone Betsy said 'Poor old Tattty, she must be worried out of her mind.'

'Don't worry,' said Annabel 'She will talk it over with her infant teacher Miss Wright in the morning and it will be a topic of conversation for days.'

'But what are we going to do about it?' asked Betsy.

'If Mr Griffiths is involved in this then something fishy is going on and we are going to have to find out about it. The first thing we need to know is why he is so keen on closing the school. Then when we know that we can work out a plan'

Actually, it didn't take much to find out about it as Mrs Raven who cleaned for the Griffiths was more than helpful over a cup of tea.

'I didn't actually hear anything you understand,' she said. 'But they were talking so loudly what can a body do. Anyway, he's gone and done old Miss Tatt in he really has. He told the Town Council they ought to close the school but what he really wants is to buy the school and live in it.'

Annabel was shocked. 'He's getting it closed so that he can buy it and live in it?'

'Yes,' said Eva Raven. 'Once it's closed the Council will

put it up for sale and since he knows all about it he'll snap it up for a bargain price.'

'Well I never,' said Annabel. 'Henry, listen to this.'

Henry who had just come in sat and listened while Eva told her story all over again.

'Who would have believed it,' said Henry.

'I must be off,' Mrs Raven rose. 'I've got to get on to my next job. Thanks for the tea Annabel. Let me know if there is anything else I can do to help.'

'Thanks Eva we'll keep in touch.'

After she had left, Annabel gazed out of the window watching the clouds race by.

'There's one way to stop this,' she said. 'And I know how to do it.'

Henry knew from long experience that once Annabel had made up her mind to do something there was no stopping her. He also knew that there was no point in asking her about it until she was ready to tell him.

The rest of the week proceeded more or less normally or so it seemed to Betsy. She had no idea what Annabel was going to do but on Monday she found out.

On Monday morning the school bus drew up in the centre of the village. It had the words 'School Bus' on the front but actually it was Sid Fellows' usual bus that made the trip to Cirencester twice a day.

Now it meant that Sid had to make two extra journeys, once in the morning to take the children to school and once in the afternoon to bring them back. Not that he minded as he liked children but he grumbled because the bus company wouldn't pay him extra for the trips.

So, Monday morning saw Sid and his bus outside the pub at Happy End waiting to take the children to Cirencester. There were anxious mothers milling around, making sure their offspring were wrapped up warm, mothers fussing, children talking excitedly about the new school, some looking frightened, some looking forward to the new adventure. Miss Tatt and Miss Wright were there as they had to accompany the children and teach them for a first trial month.

Counsellor Griffiths' son Tommy wasn't on the bus as his father was going to take him in 'the car'. The car being the latest model Rover.

'All aboard,' said Sid, hooting his horn. 'Off we go.'

Annabel who was watching the proceedings smiled quietly to herself.

The bus started off with the children waving to their parents and the parents waving back. It went about a hundred yards down the road and shuddered to a halt.

Counsellor Griffiths honked his car horn and set off to overtake the bus. As it reached exactly the same point as the bus, its engine missed a beat and stopped.

It was as though there was an invisible barrier across the road that prevented the bus and the car from going any further.

He kept pounding the steering wheel and turning the ignition key until the battery showed signs of giving up on the starter motor. Neither the bus nor his car could move an inch.

That should do it, thought Annabel, but it didn't. Counsellor Griffiths rang the garage on his mobile phone and then rang the bus company.

'We must get the children to school,' he told them. 'Send another bus immediately.'

Immediately is always a relative term but in time another bus turned up. Meanwhile the children had tumbled out of Sid's bus and were playing on the roadside. The second bus turned in the side road a little ahead of the stranded one and stood waiting for the children to board.

Annabel's spell, for that is what it was, didn't extend to the second bus and in any case she knew that it would wear off in about half an hour.

The children boarded the second bus and off they went to Cirencester accompanied by Miss Tatt and Miss Wright. No mechanic had appeared to fix the Counsellor's car so he put Tommy onto the second bus with the other children.

Three quarters of an hour later a mechanic from the garage did turn up but by that time the spell had worn off and he could find nothing wrong with the car apart from a flat battery. Sid who had been sitting patiently in his bus started the engine and drove off.

'That didn't work,' said Annabel to Betsy when she got back to the house. 'Now what?'

Meanwhile the children had arrived at their new school and were sitting in their temporary classrooms under the direction of Miss Tatt and Miss Wright..

They both agreed that they would make the best of a bad job but neither they nor the children had their hearts in it. Everyone was quietly hoping that they could go back to their own school except Tommy Griffiths who had been brainwashed to believe everything his father told him.

'I only hope Annabel can think of some way of stopping this,' Miss Tatt said to Miss Wright at their break time.

Next day the bus arrived on time but when the children had been loaded, the engine started, then stopped, then started again but wouldn't move. Eventually the replacement bus arrived and the children were again delivered late to school.

The following day the bus started normally but halfway there it turned back of its own accord and headed back to the village school. This was quite a difficult spell and it took all Annabel's attention to hold it in place. So much so that when the bus reached the village Annabel lay back in her chair totally exhausted and the spell snapped. Sid the bus driver regained control and took the children to Cirencester.

'This is no good, Mum,' said Betsy. 'You're wearing yourself out to no purpose. This isn't going to stop them.'

When Annabel recovered she thought of all sorts of things she could do like locking the classroom doors so that they couldn't get in, or making holes in the roof to let the rain in.'

'No, Mum,' said Betsy firmly. 'You have always told me the way to beat anything is to concentrate on the real problem. What is the real problem?'

Annabel thought for a moment. 'It's really about beating Counsellor Griffiths and getting our school back.'

'So,' said Betsy. 'If he is at the heart of the problem how can we get him to drop the idea of buying the school and make him want to open it again?'

'I can see that I have been looking at this the wrong way round,' said Annabel. 'But what can we do?' She looked at her daughter in despair.

'I have an idea,' said Betsy. 'Listen to this.'

* * *

That night Counsellor Griffiths had his hot chocolate as usual and went off to bed kissing his wife Griselda on the cheek. He slept on his own as Griselda said that he snored in his sleep and she couldn't put up with that.

As always he fell asleep quite easily but sometime in the middle of the night he was woken up by a moaning noise. At first, he incorporated it into the dream he was having but as it went on he gradually surfaced and realised that there was something in his room.

That something was the shadowy figure of a woman surrounded by a ghostly white light.

'I'm glad you woke up,' said the figure. 'I was just getting ready to give a horrible scream. Pity as I haven't done one of those for a long time.'

The 'ghost' was of course Annabel disguised by a white

sheet. Betsy who had been given some luminous paint for Christmas had provided the ghostly light.

'What do you want?' Counsellor G cowered back, hiding under the bedclothes.

'You,' moaned Annabel. 'I want you to come with me.'

The bedclothes flew back at Annabel's command and the bed literally tipped him out so that his nightshirt flew up over his legs.

'We are going on a trip you and I,' said Annabel.

*   *   *

Counsellor Griffiths found himself standing in the dark and deserted main room of the school with Annabel standing slightly behind him.

Witches are good at conjuring up what we now call holographic projections but what in Annabel's day was just called magic.

The scene that unfolded in front of Counsellor G's eyes was like something out of a Dickens' novel. There were ten young pupils sitting at old-fashioned school desks each bending over an exercise book laboriously copying what the teacher wrote on the board. The teacher was old, with mittens on his hands to keep them warm. The children were dressed in ragged clothes and were shivering from the cold.

Counsellor G could feel the cold himself. He turned to the 'ghost'.

'Why have you brought me here?' he asked.

'Watch and you will see,' she said in her best ghostly voice.

As they stood there, one of the pupils seemed to catch the teacher's eye. He picked up a thin flexible cane, went over to the child and after peering at his exercise book began hitting him across the shoulders with the cane.

'Here, stop that,' Counsellor Griffiths stepped forward.

'They can't see or hear you,' said Annabel. 'Just watch.'

The cane descended again, this time missing the boy's shoulders and landing on the back of his neck. He slumped to the floor catching his head of the frame of the desk. The teacher tried to haul him back on his seat.

All eyes were trained on the incident. The children looked frightened. The teacher quickly dismissed the class leaving the boy slumped in his seat. When all the children had gone, he began slapping the boy in the face to try to bring him to consciousness but without result.

'The boy is dead,' burst out Counsellor G.

The teacher thought the same as he dragged the boy over to a cupboard and shut him in.

The scene changed and they were standing in the school garden early on a misty morning. The teacher had a shovel and was digging a grave. The boy lay nearby.

'This is terrible,' said the Counsellor. 'Why hasn't someone called the police?'

'What you're seeing,' said Annabel, 'is something that happened many years ago but the boy's skeleton still lingers beneath the soil and his ghost walks the school room.'

The scene changed again and they were back in the main room. This time the desks, blackboard and all the equipment were modern. It was night time so no children were present but over in the corner was the ghost of the boy who had been killed his head bent over a desk. As Counsellor G took a step backwards the boy looked up.

'He can see us,' he gasped.

'Of course,' said Annabel. He sees what we see but is doomed to stay forever in this classroom until someone releases his soul from the body in the garden.'

As they watched, the boy got up and came over to them.

'Can you help me sir?' the ghost said politely. 'I can't rest until my body is buried in hallowed ground. And I am so tired of being earth bound.'

Counsellor G was about to reply when the ghostly image faded and he found himself alone in the cold dark classroom. Annabel had also quietly withdrawn making sure that the classroom door was unlocked so that he would be able to find his way out.

He looked around for Annabel and called out, 'Aren't you going to take me home to my bed.' But there was no Annabel to answer him.

So, with no shoes on his feet and clad only in his nightshirt he stumbled out into the darkness, the cold wind whipping through the thin garment.

'This can't be a dream,' he thought. 'It's too real.'

He discovered just how real it was when he reached home and found the front door locked. He threw some small pebbles at his wife's window to wake her up. Eventually the window opened and a bleary eyed Griselda looked down.

'What's going on,' she called.

'It's me,' said Counsellor G.

'What are you doing down there in your nightshirt. You'll catch your death. Come in this instant.'

'I can't,' he wailed. 'At least not until you open the door.'

Grumbling, his wife put on a dressing gown and came down. She opened the door and a cold and miserable man fell into the house.

'What have you been up to?' she demanded.

'Never mind woman,' he snapped. 'I'll tell you in the morning. Get off to bed.'

Such was the nature of their relationship that, after locking the door, she did.

Counsellor Griffiths poured himself a large tot of whisky and subsided into an easy chair. The fiery liquid gradually began to thaw him out and he fell asleep.

*　*　*

Annabel reached home, let herself in, changed out of her spooky costume and went up to bed. Henry was snoring quietly as she slipped in her side of the bed.

'A good night's work, I think.' She turned over and went to sleep.

*　*　*

Next morning Counsellor Griffiths woke with a start. At first, he was unable to take in his surroundings. Soon the memory of the murder he had witnessed came back to him. He jumped up and went to the telephone then realised that he was still in his nightshirt.

Wash and breakfast first, he thought and went off to the bathroom. By the time he had finished and come down again his wife was making breakfast. Tommy, his son, was already at the breakfast table and although his wife looked questioningly at him he said he would explain later when Tommy was at school.

He had already abandoned the idea of taking him to Cirencester in the car and now left him to join the bus with the other children.

When Tommy left, he gave a brief explanation to his wife who obviously didn't believe a word, and rang the Police Station at Barrow Magna where Sergeant Fred Fossett was just making himself a cup of tea.

'Right you are sir,' said Fred almost saluting the phone. 'I'll come over and bring young Ted with me.'

Young Ted was probably older that Sergeant Fossett but he was still an acting constable.

'Come on out of there, young Ted,' said Fred going over to the station's only jail cell. When on duty they took it in turns to sleep in the cell to be available twenty four hours a day although Fred sometimes wondered why they bothered. Last night it had been Ted's turn to be on night duty. Fred had come in just in time to take Counsellor G's phone call.

'And bring that shovel with you,' he said. 'It looks as if we may have to do a bit of digging.'

Ted slept in his clothes so it didn't take long before they were in the police car and off to Happy End. Ted wanted to switch the siren on but Fred wouldn't let him.

'This is a stealth operation,' he said. 'We may be digging up a body.'

By the time they arrived at the school Counsellor G was there and in the strange way that people always get wind of something going on a small crowd was beginning to gather.

Three hours later, after digging up most of the school garden, Ted rested on his shovel and scratched his head. 'There ain't no body here,' he said. He had turned up a collection of old tin cans, a dead bird, bits of an old vase, and what looked like a Roman coin.

'That might be worth something,' he said.

'Treasure trove that is, we'll have to report it,' said Sergeant Fossett.

'Well sir,' turning to Counsellor G. 'I reckon someone's been having you on. There's no body here as far as we can tell.'

The crowd was beginning to disperse as it looked as if the fun was over.

'Thank you, Sergeant,' he said. 'I'm sorry to have troubled you.'

'No trouble I'm sure, sir,' said Fred Fossett. 'Of course, I'll have to ask you to come down to the Station to make a formal statement.'

'Is that strictly necessary?' asked Counsellor G.

'Oh yes sir, very necessary,' said Fred and thought, especially since you've wasted our time all morning and my missus is going to be mad at me for being late for lunch.

*   *   *

Annabel had been part of the crowd that watched Ted dig up the school garden. In fact, it was she who had spread the word round the village and caused the crowd to gather.

'He ought to feel pretty shamefaced after this and what with the idea of a ghost in the house he wanted to live in, perhaps he will give up the idea,' she said to Henry when she got back home.

'I'm not so sure,' said Henry. 'That Counsellor Griffiths is a stubborn old fool. When he gets an idea in his head there's no stopping him.'

But, he was wrong. Some days later the news was all round the village that the school was to be reopened. Miss Tatt came round to see Annabel.

'I don't know how you did it,' she said, 'Counsellor Griffiths apparently spoke out at the Council meeting and they are going to reopen the school. Everything will be back to normal.'

The true explanation filtered down to Annabel through Olive Garner at the Post Office.

'Counsellor Griffiths told the vicar that the reason he spoke up to have the school reopened was his son Tommy.

Apparently Tommy liked the idea of stepping across from his house to the school and didn't like the idea of bussing all that way to Cirencester every day.'

'I wonder,' said Annabel to her husband. 'I wonder if that's the true reason or did his ghostly encounter have anything to do with it?'

'We shall never know,' said Henry. 'But you gave him a fright that night. I wish I had been there to see it.'

10

The Village Fete

'**W**in a pig. Three balls a penny.'

'Rollup Ladies and Gentlemen. See the amazing Zenda. She wrestles with snakes. Terrifying, daring. Rollup, rollup.'

The village fete was in full swing on the vicarage lawn. The 'Try Your Strength' machine was fully occupied by the young men of the village while the girls and women queued up to have their fortunes told by Madame Vera.

Inside the small tent Annabel lightly disguised with a gypsy headdress, veil and a shawl was poring over her crystal ball. Sitting opposite her was a young woman from Barrow Magna.

'I see a tall dark stranger,' Annabel said, her voice muffled by the veil. 'You are going on a journey. What is it, Betsy? Can't you see I'm telling this young lady's fortune.'

Betsy had popped into the tent. 'Sorry, Mum, I didn't mean to disturb you but Dad said to remind you to see him at the plant stall at half past three.' She popped out as quickly as she had popped in.

'Sorry for the interruption, my dear but that's about it. The crystal has gone dim. That will be fifty pence please.'

While the young lady was fiddling in her handbag to find the money, Annabel sat back and mopped her brow.

This fake fortune telling is harder than the real thing, she thought. Maybe I ought to tell them what I really see in the crystal.

It was about twenty past three and the queue outside her tent seemed never ending. She needed a break but there was no one to relieve her. What should she do?

The next person who came in bent low hiding her face in the dim light.

Annabel looked at the figure sharply. 'Mabel Todd, is that you?'

Mabel shyly lifted her face.

'I thought I would just pop in for a chat,' she said. 'Not really for a fortune telling.'

'You don't know how welcome you are,' said Annabel. 'Now just you put on this headdress, shawl and veil and become me for a little while. Tell some fortunes while I go and see Henry.'

Mabel twittered nervously, 'I couldn't, I really couldn't. I don't know how to tell fortunes.'

'Of course you do. Just tell them something about their

love life. Make it up. Tell them that the next few weeks will mark a change in their life. That sort of thing. You can't go wrong.'

She gently pushed Mabel into her chair and put the Madame Vera clothing on her.

'Oh, and don't forget to look into the crystal ball while you say these things. Very impressive.'

Annabel quickly made her way out of the tent telling the next person in the queue to go in.

* * *

Henry, Annabel's husband, was fussing round the plant stall as she came over.

'Going well, Henry?' she asked.

'Not too bad,' he replied. 'It was a waste of time bringing these big shrubs. All they seem to want are the pot plants.'

'It's not the same as the Saturday market in Barrow,' she said. 'Mostly they are here to enjoy themselves. The shrubs will sell on Saturday. Take them over then.'

'You are right I'm sure,' Henry mopped his brow. 'Anyway thanks for coming over. I'll go and get us both a cup of tea. Back in a jiffy.'

Annabel nodded and went over to an old lady who was examining a large tradescanthia.

'Lovely specimen that,' she said. 'A bargain at a pound.'

The old lady looked up startled, put the plant down and moved off quickly.

'Perhaps fortune telling is easier than selling plants,' she said to herself.

Henry came back with cups of tea for both of them. Annabel told him about the fortune telling while they drank.

'It's never ending,' she said. 'And some of the things I see in that crystal I daren't tell them.'

'Why not?' asked Henry. 'That's what they have come for isn't it?'

'Yes, but they don't know I can do it for real so I tell them all this 'you are going on a long journey' stuff and they lap it up.'

'Well try telling them what you really see for a change and see what happens.'

*　　*　　*

Annabel went back to her tent where Mabel Todd was telling the next client that she had an unhappy love life but that it would improve.

'That's good to hear,' said the red-faced country woman. I've been a widow these twelve years so anything would be an improvement. Do you see a man involved by any chance?'

Mabel became flustered and looked up at Annabel.

'Yes,' said Annabel looking in the crystal. 'There quite clearly is a man. I see him chopping wood for you and piling the logs up in a basket.'

'That will be Caleb Wilson. I know he's sweet on me. Thank you Annabel.' She put her fifty pence down on the table and rushed out obviously delighted.

Did you actually see a man in the crystal,' asked Mabel removing her veil and handing over the disguise to Annabel.

'Of course my dear,' said Annabel. 'Didn't you see it?'

'All I saw were some weird shapes. Can I go now?'

'Yes and thank you for helping me. Now I had better get back to work.'

The next person in the tent was old Mrs Twitchett from the house down at the end of the village.

Annabel peered into the crystal. At first it was dark and then Annabel saw Mrs Twitchett receiving a letter with what looked like a foreign stamp on it. As she watched, the old lady opened the letter and read its contents then the crystal went dark again.

She told Mrs Twitchett exactly what she had seen.

'That'll be Tom my eldest boy,' she looked excited. 'I haven't heard from him in months. Can you read what's in the letter?'

'I'll try,' said Annabel and concentrated on the crystal again. She was just about to say that she could tell no more when she saw a taxi drawing up outside Mrs Twitchett's house. A young man and woman got out and she could see Mrs T welcoming them into the house.

'Is your Tom married?' she asked.

'Not that I know of,' she replied.

'Well, I think the letter will be good news. Tom is either married or going to get married and he is bringing her to see you.'

'That's wonderful. I don't know how you do it Annabel,' she said.

Perhaps, thought Annabel as Mrs Twitchett left. Perhaps I should tell them what I see in the crystal. It's certainly better than making it up.

There was a lull in the proceedings and as no-one came into the tent Annabel got up and looked outside. The queue had dispersed and apart from Tony Raven and a group of his friends standing around the 'Try Your Strength' machine which stood next to her tent there was no-one about. She went back inside putting a cloth carefully over her crystal ball.

The ball had been handed down to her by her mother who had it from her mother. As far as Annabel knew, it had been in her family of witches for generations being handed down through the female line. Annabel used it not for telling fortunes but for concentrating her thoughts when someone came to her in trouble. She knew that it was capable of letting her see things, often things that were at a great distance. She was also conscious that it had other powers, some of which she had no knowledge of.

She woke with a start as someone came into the tent.

'Miss Tatt, come in,' she said. 'I must have dozed off. I've been telling fortunes all afternoon. It's a tiring business.'

'I wish you would tell my fortune,' said Miss Tatt. After that business with Counsellor Griffiths trying to close the school I'm all at sixes and sevens.'

'He didn't manage it did he,' said Annabel. 'Although

I don't think we have heard the last of that gentleman. He's trouble if ever I saw it.'

She drew the cloth gently from the crystal.

'There's a very strong reaction here,' she said. 'Let me see what I can tell you.'

'Of course I don't believe in this sort of thing,' said Miss Tatt nervously.

'Don't worry there is nothing to be afraid of.'

Annabel stared at the picture unfolding in front of her eyes.

Miss Tatt was coming out of Annabel's tent. She could see Tony Raven and his friends still standing round the 'Try Your Strength' machine.

'This must be now,' she murmured to herself.

'What was that?' snapped Miss Tatt.

Annabel had forgotten that teachers have especially sharp ears tuned to hear whispering in class.

'Nothing,' she said soothingly. 'Let me see.'

The scene in the crystal changed and there was Miss Tatt standing in front of the bric-a-brac stall examining a small blue vase. Tony and his friends were still in the background. The scene changed and there was Miss Tatt lying on the ground with people rushing towards her.

'Get the doctor,' she thought she heard someone say.

Pull yourself together, she thought. The crystal isn't fitted with sound. At least I don't think so. A feeling of dread flowed over her.

Miss Tatt was looking at her expectantly.

'Is something wrong?' she asked.

'No, nothing,' Annabel said hesitantly. 'I think the crystal must be having an off moment. I'm afraid there is nothing I can tell you. There will be no charge for the consultation.'

Miss Tatt looked surprised, closed her bag with a snap and got up to go.

'Well really, Annabel, I do think you could have at least made something up like a tall dark stranger coming into my life. Well good day to you.' She stormed out.

Annabel sat there dazed. Betsy popped her head round the tent flap.

'What's the matter, Mum, you look as if you have seen a ghost?'

'May be I have, may be I have,' said her mother. 'But I'm not sure what to do.'

She explained to Betsy what she had seen.

'I think Miss Tatt is going to have an accident at the fete,' she said.

'What sort of accident?' asked Betsy.

'That's the trouble, I don't know,' said Annabel.

'Look into the crystal again and see if it will tell you,' said Betsy.

They both stared at the crystal but apart from dark moving shapes they could see nothing.

'Betsy,' said Annabel. 'Go outside and ask Tony and his friends if they would keep an eye on Miss Tatt for me. They might be able to prevent whatever is going to happen.'

'Right Mum,' Betsy went out quickly.

When she came back, it was to report that Tony had agreed to shadow Miss Tatt until she left the fete.

'Almost time to pack up anyway,' said Annabel. 'I promised the vicar I would go over to help him distribute prizes for the races.'

She took the crystal ball and put it gently into its padded box, then drawing off her headdress and veil she gave them to Betsy to put in the truck which was parked in the yard outside the vicarage.

'Okay, Mum. See you at the prize giving. Betsy went out carefully holding the box in both hands. They both knew how valuable it was.

Annabel crossed the lawn towards the dais that had been built just outside the vicarage French windows. On the way, she noticed Miss Tatt standing by the bric-a-brac stall examining a blue vase while Tony and his friends hovered in the background. She nodded at them and went over to the Vicar who was hunting among things on the table at the side of the dais.

'I could have sworn I put my glasses down on the table,' he said fumbling around.

'They are on your nose Reverend,' said Annabel helpfully.

'Oh dear,' he said putting his hand up to feel them. 'I am getting rather absentminded you know.'

Annabel smiled at him. 'We all are, but don't you fret, let's get on with the prize giving.'

The first prize went to young Jason Wilkins for winning the potato race. Jason a red faced youngster, collected his prize, a bat and ball set, and displayed it proudly to his mother. The prize giving went on but Annabel's mind was half on Miss Tatt.

'Don't be silly,' she said to herself. 'Tony Raven is a good lad and he's looking after her.'

In fact, Tony and his friends were causing Miss Tatt some discomfort. She would move to another stall only to find Tony right behind her.

'Are you following me?' she asked him sharply.

Tony couldn't say anything because Betsy had asked him not to, so he blurted out, 'Sorry, Miss Tatt. I didn't realise it was you.'

'Go away,' she said irritably. 'And take your little friends with you.'

They made off towards the refreshment tent.

'What do we do now,' asked one of the boys.

'Not much we can do,' said Tony. 'Only don't tell Betsy, she will be furious.'

So Miss Tatt was left alone to wander her way past the stalls being greeted by friends and parents who all wanted to stop and chat to her and ask how their 'little Johnny' was getting on.

Meanwhile Annabel knew nothing of this and when the prize giving was at an end went over to Henry who was packing up his plants. He and Betsy were carrying them on trays out to the truck.

As she went to help them she caught sight of Miss Tatt coming out of the refreshment tent.

'Everything all right?' she called.

'Fine,' replied Miss Tatt coming over. 'I had to chase that Tony Raven off. He and his friends were following me about but nothing else. Why?'

'No reason,' said Annabel quickly going back to Henry's stall.

In the truck afterwards Annabel was very quiet.

'What's the matter Mum?' asked Betsy.

'Nothing much,' she said. 'It's just that I have never known the crystal to be wrong. Miss Tatt should have had an accident but obviously she didn't.'

'Let's get home and put the kettle on,' said Henry. 'I've got to go back later to help dismantle the stalls but for now a cup of tea will help take your mind off it. Mistakes can happen you know.'

Annabel's mind was not at rest.

'I'm coming back with you afterwards just to make sure,' she said.

They unloaded the truck, had a cup of tea and a piece of cake and then set off back to the vicarage. As they came near to the church a figure lurched into the road in front of them.

'Look out,' Annabel clutched at Henry's arm as he swerved hard causing the truck to mount the grass verge.

'It's Tatty,' said Betsy. 'Is she hurt?'

'No,' said Henry. 'Lucky the truck has got good brakes.'

They were all rather shaken but Miss Tatt didn't seem to notice them as she walked on towards the vicarage.

'I think she is short sighted,' said Betsy with that

condescending attitude of youth towards anyone slightly older than themselves.

'At least she is still all right,' said Annabel.

They found an army of helpers on the lawn taking down stalls, trestle tables and moving seats and leftovers.

'The tent people will come on Monday,' said the vicar. 'If we can get everything into the big refreshment tent they will take it all away.'

The fete on the vicarage lawn took place every year the first Saturday in June. The vicar, the Reverend Alistair Harding had been organising it for a number of years and had got it down to a fine art. The proceeds from the various activities, less any expenses, would go to a number of charities decided by the Parochial Church Council.

The vicar was quite cheerful.

'It didn't rain and I think we have made as much as last year,' he told Annabel as she helped him stack chairs in the tent.

Miss Tatt and various other helpers were packing things up, putting things away and generally clearing the lawn. There was very little rubbish about thanks to the vicar's foresight in placing bins around the lawn at strategic intervals.

Annabel was helping Henry move one of these to the black bin bags over by the edge of the lawn when there was a commotion on the other side.

'Fetch a doctor,' she heard, and knew immediately what it was.

'Miss Tatt,' she cried and set off with Henry towards the cluster of people.

When they got nearer, there she was lying on the ground just as Annabel had seen it in the crystal. It looked as if a pole from one of the stalls had fallen and struck her a glancing blow. Fortunately, it was a wooden one, not metal, and as they came up to her she was just getting up off the ground. To everyone's surprise, she was clutching a small child in her arms.

'She was walking past when the stall fell on her. I just managed to snatch her away but the pole hit me.' She gave the child to its mother who rushed up to Miss Tatt almost in tears.

Miss Tatt looked a bit groggy and had a bruise on her arm but she smiled valiantly.

'Come over to the refreshment tent and sit down for a bit.' Annabel drew her away from the crowd who were congratulating her on her rapid action in saving the child. In the tent Annabel drew a container from one of her voluminous pockets.

'Put this on,' she said. 'It will ease the pain and draw the bruise out.'

'What is it?' asked Miss Tatt weakly as reaction was now setting in.

'It's an old remedy passed on by my mother from her mother before her. You'll see, it will do the trick.'

As Annabel smoothed the cream on to Miss Tatt's arm, she said 'I know this can't be true but it feels better already.'

'Thank your lucky stars nothing is broken,' said Annabel. 'Rescuing children at your time of life. Still it was a brave act.'

To herself she said 'And I saw this in the crystal and didn't do the right thing.'

Later when she told Betsy, she said 'You can't blame yourself Mum. You didn't know when or what was going to happen. The crystal only showed you the accident and it turned out all right in the end.'

Postman's Knock

It was three o'clock in the afternoon when Jack Jennings walked into Henry Witchell's Plant Centre.

'Is Annabel about?' he asked.

'Unusual time for delivering, Jack,' said Henry.

Jack Jennings was the local postman and his usual routine was to start at one end of the village at about 7.15am and finish his round at the Post Office Stores usually at the latest by 11am.

'This isn't a delivery,' said Jack. 'I just wanted to have a chat with Annabel. Is she in?'

'She's about somewhere,' said Henry. 'Hang on I'll see if I can find her.'

Then, seeing Betsy he asked, 'Seen your Mum anywhere?'

Betsy called back, 'She's over at the 'witches den'.'

Henry grinned at Jack. 'That's what we call her workroom.

She's got one of the old potting sheds. Turned it into quite a laboratory for her experiments she has.'

He pointed the way through the first polytunnel to a row of more permanent buildings at the back. 'Just go across Jack. She will be there.'

Jack picked his way through the masses of growing plants then through a polytunnel full of geranium cuttings and out at the far side to a substantial wooden hut.

He knocked on the door, which swung open at his touch.

'Come in, Jack,' said Annabel without looking up. She was heating a brownish liquid in what looked suspiciously like a witch's cauldron.

'How did you know it was me,' asked Jack.

'We witches know all sorts of things,' said Annabel with a smile. 'Actually I saw you coming across the yard. Well, what can I do for you? Sit down for a minute, you look fair whacked.'

Jack looked round for somewhere to sit but books, pots, or pans occupied all three chairs in the room.

'Hang on a minute.' Annabel carefully lifted the books off the nearest chair and placed them on the workbench. Jack drew the chair up to where Annabel was working.

'There we are,' she said. 'Excuse me if I go on stirring this. I can't leave it now it's reached the critical stage.'

'Is it some mystic potion?' asked Jack.

Annabel laughed. 'Bless you, no. I'm just making vegetable soup and I want to catch it before it boils. Once it's simmering I can take my eyes off it for a bit.'

Jack sat patiently until Annabel seemed satisfied. She cleared another chair and drew it up beside him.

'Now tell me, Jack, what's the matter. We don't often get a visit from you after your regular round.'

Jack fidgeted with his cap. 'You see it's like this.'

He looked uncomfortable. 'I don't hardly know how to begin,' he said.

Annabel leant towards him and patted him on the shoulder.

'Just let it all out,' she said. 'You will feel better if you do.'

'Well it's like this,' he began. 'As you know I gets dropped off every morning by van at about a quarter past seven. Then I walks round the village, rain or shine delivering the mail.

'I finish my round anytime after about half past ten when I drops into the Post Office to pick up the mail. Mrs Garner gives me a cup of tea and a piece of cake before the van picks me up again and takes me back to the sorting office in Barrow Magna.'

'So far so good,' said Annabel. 'What's wrong with that? It seems very straightforward.'

'Well,' said Jack. 'The people are getting me down. The round is all right and up until recently, I have really enjoyed my work. I get rained on, the sun beats down and I go out in all weathers but it's the people and their dogs.'

'You had better explain,' said Annabel.

'Take the dogs. There's a lot of dogs in Happy End and some of them are very nice and greet me friendly like but there's others that would bite you as soon as look at you.

'There one particular one out at old Heathcote's place on the edge of the village. That devil waits for me every morning. It hides behind the wall then when I opens the gate it jumps out at me, grabs my trouser leg and won't let go. I've told Mr Heathcote about it but he just says it's playful and he won't keep it in.

'That's not the only one. Sometimes I'm fair afraid to put post through people's letter boxes for fear of getting bitten.'

'What about the people, Jack?' asked Annabel. 'What's wrong with the people?'

Jack sat silent for a minute thinking.

'It's more one person,' he said. 'John Pike. He fair gets on my nerves. Always picking on me. He's like the dogs, always lying in wait for me. Always complaining about the post. Accuses me of losing letters or not delivering on time.

'I can't understand it. He always used to be such a nice fellow. Always had a good word and his wife often offered me a cup of tea on a cold morning. Now you don't get a civil word out of him since his wife left him.'

'Well there it is,' said Annabel. 'If he's now on his own of course he's grumpy. No woman to care for him. Didn't I hear that she had run off with some gypsy fellow that came in with the Summer Fair?'

'Yes, I heard that too,' said Jack. 'I can see why he would be upset but there's no need to take it out on me.'

'Perhaps he's taking it out on everyone,' said Annabel. 'Have you checked?'

'No I haven't,' said Jack. 'It's a good idea. I'll find out.'

He put his head in his hands. 'It's not just him, it's everyone,' he said.

Annabel sat and thought for a minute.

'What you need is a pick-me-up my lad,' she said. 'I have got just the thing for you.'

She went over to the shelves at the back of the room and brought back a bottle containing a brownish coloured liquid.

'Take this three times a day for a week and you will begin to feel your old self again.'

She labelled the bottle 'Take a spoonful three times a day to be taken in water.'

She handed Jack the bottle. 'I've got something else for you,' she said delving into a cupboard. 'I want you to sprinkle a few drops of this on the end of your trousers before you go on your round. You will probably only have to do it once. It should put the dogs off.'

Jack took the stopper out of the bottle and gave it a sniff.

'What is it?' he asked. 'It don't half pong.'

'Don't you worry about that,' said Annabel. 'It's quite harmless but it will stop them attacking. Now off with you and I want you to report back on progress in two days time.'

Later that evening when Annabel, Henry and Betsy were sitting round the fire, Annabel told them Jack's story.

'He went off like a two year old,' she said.

'But what did you give him?' asked Betsy.

'Nothing harmful,' said Annabel. 'The medicine was just coloured water. The start of the real cure was to let him talk about it. The dog deterrent is guaranteed to stop any dog

in its tracks at ten yards. I only hope his missus can stand
the smell but I'm sure he changes out of his uniform when
he gets home.'

Then she looked thoughtful. 'I think I'd better take a
look at John Pike and find out what's going on.

* * *

John Pike, blissfully unaware of any interest in him, was
digging his garden trying to get his late potatoes in.

'Drat and damn,' he said as his fork kept binding on the
stony soil. Instead of lifting the stones out and preparing the
ground properly, he just went on drating them which had
no effect whatsoever.

A hooded figure, looking like Red Riding Hood, carrying
a basket, came up the lane to his cottage. It stopped and
looked at him toiling in his garden. It was Annabel. She
pushed back the hood and wished him a good morning.

'Humph,' he said. 'A good morning for some but not
for me.'

Not to be beaten Annabel laid her basket down and
folded back the cloth.

'I've brought you some fresh baked rolls and some cake
John. Now your Molly has gone away I thought you might
like some goodies.'

'Thanks but no thanks,' he said, leaning on his spade.

'I don't take charity from no-one although the thought
is most welcome,' he said with an ill grace.

Annabel wasn't to be put off. 'Invite me in for a bit, John. I've got something I want to ask you.'

'Like as not you can ask me out here,' he said. 'The place isn't fit to be seen by the likes of you Annabel and that's a fact.'

'That's what I thought,' she said sailing towards the door. 'I think you need a bit of help.'

He made a feeble attempt to stop her but Annabel had already gone in.

She looked around aghast. 'You need more than a bit of help I'm thinking.'

The room was a tip. Dirty plates piled in the sink, dirty clothes strewn around the room, dust and dirt everywhere.

Annabel drew her hand across the sideboard. It came up black with soot.

'You and me's going to have a talk,' she said and lifting the accumulated rubbish off the settee she sat down and patted the seat next to her. 'Come and sit down here.'

John, still in his gardening clothes, his hands stained with soil, sat obediently by her side.

'Now tell me all about it,' she said.

Like all powerful witches, she could bend people to her will such that no-one exposed to that sharp tone and eagle eye dared to disobey her and John was no exception.

'It's like this,' he said, and soon he was pouring it all out into Annabel's sympathetic ear.

Molly, his wife of many years had suddenly taken off with a gypsy who had come to the village with the Summer Fair.

'Almost as though he had bewitched her,' he said. 'It were'nt like her at all and we've been married these fifteen years.'

'You don't have any children do you, John,' said Annabel gently.

'Molly didn't hold with that sort of thing,' John mumbled. 'I'd have liked em but she didn't want to be bothered. So why she ran off I don't know.'

'First we've got to get your place shipshape,' said Annabel. 'Then we'll have to think about this. Me and Betsy will come up tomorrow and give you a bit of a spring clean. You get yourself shaved and spruced up for when we come. One thing you could do is to give me something of Molly's so that I can take a look in my crystal ball.'

He found Annabel a scarf that belonged to Molly and she tucked it away carefully in her pocket.

'I'll leave the basket of goodies for you then, John,' she said putting it on the table. John Pike changed from a grumpy old man to a meek one. If he had been a dog he would have rolled over and waggled his legs in the air.

'That reminds me,' said Annabel. 'Where's old Spot, your dog. He doesn't seem to be around?'

'I had to take him to the Dog's Home in Barrow Magna. He fretted so much when Molly went. I couldn't stop him howling. Fair drove me crazy he did, so I took him over to Barrow. They said they would find him a good home.'

* * *

Annabel got back from doing her Little Red Riding Hood act, sat down, and thought, that man is never going to change unless he gets his Molly back. What's the best thing to do? She drew her crystal ball towards her and stared into it.

There is a mistaken belief that you can see into the present, future or past with a crystal ball and this view is promoted by clairvoyants, mediums and others. Actually, all it does is to concentrate the thoughts of the person using it. You might just as well use a bowl of tomato soup or a stick of celery.

Holding Molly's scarf in her hand she stared into the crystal letting her mind relax. At first, the crystal showed her scenes of Happy End but there was nothing there. Then widening her search to Barrow Magna, she felt a tingle. In her mind's eye, projected onto the crystal she could see a baker's shop and there behind the counter was Molly serving a customer.

'Not so far away after all,' murmured Annabel to herself. 'Right, tomorrow we shall pay a visit.'

* * *

As luck would have it, Henry was driving into Barrow Magna the next day to deliver some plants to the school. They were having an open day and wanted plants to edge the platform. Annabel went with him.

There was only one baker's shop in Barrow Magna.

Jackson's the Bakers had a few tables set at one side of the shop for the locals to meet and take tea and cakes. Annabel arranged to meet Henry there after he had finished his delivery.

In the meantime she went into the shop, sat down at a vacant table and studied the menu. A waitress came over to take her order. It was Molly.

Annabel looked up. 'Molly, this is a surprise finding you here.'

Molly looked shamefaced. 'Hallo, Annabel. We don't often see you in these parts.'

'Just dropped in for a cup of tea and a scone. I'm meeting Henry here when he's finished his delivery.'

'I'll take your order then,' said Molly, writing it on a little pad and retreating quickly behind the counter.

So, that's the size of it, thought Annabel.

Another waitress brought her tea and scone and it was obvious that Molly was going to stay out of her way.

A little persuasion is needed here, she thought. Very well.

She concentrated on Molly's back which was visible behind the counter.

A moment later Molly came flying over as though her feet were carrying her without permission.

'Sit down for a minute. Take the load off your feet,' she said, although take the load off your mind was what she meant.

Molly looked very distressed.

'I daren't sit down,' she said. 'The manageress Mrs

Mangham has got eyes in the back of her head and she don't like us hobnobbing with the customers.'

'Stand up then and tell me all about it. You look as if it would do you good to get it off your chest.'

Fortunately, there was no-one else within earshot, but even so Molly lowered her voice, speaking so softly that Annabel could only just hear her.

'It's like this,' she said.

Her story was a simple one. She had tired of cooking and cleaning for John. She never went anywhere except the Post Office Stores for food.

'John never thinks of anything outside of himself and work. All he wants to do of an evening is sit down with a pipe and watch telly.'

Annabel nodded sympathetically.

'Along comes this gypsy and he rather swept me off my feet. He was so romantic, telling me of different places he had visited, things he had done. Well I went with him and left poor John. I wish I hadn't for it was all lies. We took rooms in Barrow Magna that I paid for out of my small savings. Oh, he was a devil that one. All he wanted was my money and when that ran out, he left me. Left me with no money to pay the rent. What could I do? I couldn't go back to John. The disgrace of it and what would the village say. So I stayed here and got this job. The money's not much but it's a good job and I'm managing to keep body and soul together.

'I've talked too long. She's looking at me. I've got to go.'

She quickly walked back to the counter and started serving another customer.

Annabel sat there eating her scone and drinking her tea.

Soon Henry came in, looked around and seeing her sitting at the table headed over and sat down heavily beside her.

'That was quite a thing,' he said. 'Not only did they want me to deliver the plants they also wanted me to arrange them and some of those potted plants are a fair weight.'

Annabel ordered him a cup of tea. 'No scones for you,' she said. 'You need to watch your weight.'

Henry grinned and patted his ample stomach. 'You're right as usual,' he said. 'Although I doubt if one scone would have made much difference.'

'Don't forget,' said Annabel, 'this isn't a social occasion. We've got work to do here.'

'You mean the Molly problem. Did you locate her?'

'She's over there. No don't look,' and then, 'look now. She's turned her back.'

Henry looked quickly over his shoulder.

'I can't tell you the whole story here, but we have got to get her back to her John.'

'Why?' asked Henry. 'She left him. He's much happier on his own.'

'That's just like a man,' said Annabel. 'He isn't happy and neither is she. We have got to get them back together as soon as we can.'

'Well we can't drag her out of the shop screaming,' said

Henry. 'So what do we do?'

'We apply a little psychology and maybe a little witchery but let's go home now.'

Annabel paid the bill and said goodbye to Molly.

'I'll be in touch,' she said.

Molly looked tearful but nodded and turned away.

Annabel sat in thought on the way home and Henry knew that she was laying her plans.

* * *

Next day a little dog walked in through the open door of Jackson's shop. The manageress Mrs Mangham looked at it in horror.

'Dogs are not allowed in here,' she said sternly. 'Get out, get out.'

The dog took no notice and trotted up to Mollie who had just been serving a customer.

'Why it's Spot,' she said, as the dog sat up and begged.

'You shouldn't be here Spot,' she said fondling its ears.

Mrs Mangham came over.

'Is this your dog?' she asked.

'In a manner of speaking,' Mollie replied. 'It actually belongs to my husband. I can't think how it got here.'

'Well, get it out of here fast,' Mrs Mangham shouted. 'I don't care whose dog it is, just get it out.'

'Yes, Mrs Mangham,' Mollie caught hold of Spot's collar and guided the dog out of the shop.

A truck drew up beside her. It was Henry.

'Hallo Mollie,' he said leaning over and opening the door. 'Can I give you a lift?'

Mollie was a bit bewildered by the turn of events but was soon seated beside Henry with Spot on the floor at her feet.

'How come you were there to pick me up?' she asked.

Henry thought 'I can't tell her how Annabel managed to get the dog's home to release the dog and carefully timed it so that I would be passing the door at exactly the right time.'

'I was just coming back from Barrow School,' he said. 'They have a lot of my plants there for their open day tomorrow and I wanted to make sure they watered them properly.'

'Oh,' said Mollie. 'I suppose it's all right. I don't know how Spot got to Barrow but we had better take him back to John.'

They arrived at John Pike's cottage where he was in the garden digging.

'I'll wait for you if you want to go back,' said Henry.

Spot bounded up the garden path, leapt into the vegetable patch and jumped up at John. He looked round and saw Mollie standing outside Henry's truck.

'Mollie,' he said. 'You've brought Spot back and yourself as well.' He stumbled down the path towards her.

Forgetting his earthy hands he gave her a big hug and a long kiss.

'It's good to have you back, love,' he said stroking her hair.

Mollie, always a quick thinker, hugged him tight and said, 'It's good to be back.'

Henry observing the tableau of man, wife and dog quietly slipped the truck into gear and drove off towards home.

* * *

That went off very well,' said Annabel. 'I suppose now they will live happy ever after.'

Next day there was a knock at the door. Annabel opened it and there on the doorstep was Jack the postman.

'No post for you today,' he said 'But I just wanted to thank you. That medicine of yours worked a fair treat. John Pike is a different person after I took your medicine and I've had no more trouble with dogs since I sprinkled that stuff on my trousers. Mind you, the missus won't have my uniform trousers in the house. I have to leave them in the shed and go out and change into them in the morning. I must tell you its a bit nippy out in the cold first thing in the morning. Still it's worth it. Thanks to you I'm a changed man.'

Annabel smiled to herself, thinking it's not just you who are changed. Molly, John and Spot are back together again so all is pretty right with the world.

Annabel goes to the Circus

When Circus de la Lune came to Barrow Magna it set off a chain of events that led to Annabel being heralded as saviour of the circus.

The name of the circus came originally from friends of the man who set it up. Everyone said that Jimmy Jessop was loony to want to start a circus so he adopted the name to make his circus sound mysterious.

As a child he had wanted to run away to a circus but was prevented from doing so by his mother who apprenticed him to a bootmaker in Harrogate.

Jimmy was a bright lad and soon he was promoted, eventually taking over the business from his aging employer. Helped by a natural flair he expanded the business, opened shops and developed a thriving concern but he never lost his love of the circus. Whenever one came to Harrogate he was always there. Sometimes in his office he could be seen at his desk juggling with four balls at once. If visitors were expected he would quickly hide them in a drawer.

His business was so successful that he eventually decided to put in a management team and to fulfil his lifelong ambition while he was still young enough to enjoy it. So Circus de la Lune was born.

He soon discovered that it wasn't as easy as he had thought. Finding circus acts was not a problem as it seemed that in Harrogate and the surrounding area there were circus acts, trapeze artists, and people who wanted to be clowns in great abundance. No, the real problems came in finding and buying a big top, the tent in which to house the acts. As for the animals that every circus must have, where do you find an elephant, liberty horses, lions and tigers?

Starting a circus from scratch was not easy but Jimmy was always a man for a challenge. He was fortunate to come across a circus that was just closing down so he got a big top, lorries and equipment at what the proprietor said was a bargain price but to Jimmy it seemed like a fortune. He also interviewed and took on some of the acts including Miss BB and her performing horses, a team of high stepping stallions that he thought was really great.

After the deal had been done the previous owner stood there scratching his head.

'I don't know why you want to take this lot on, lad,' he said. 'It's nowt but a load of trouble. You'll see.'

And see he did. The tasks he had to perform, like keeping

all the artists together as a team, booking places for them to perform, feeding and housing everyone. There were hundred's of things to consider. He was helped in this by the previous owner who advised him on the best spots to book and who to approach.

'But circus's are dead,' he said. 'You would be better off keeping your money. Mark my words.'

At the time Jimmy didn't think much about this but later he wished he had paid more attention and asked more questions.

At last, Circus de la Lune was on the road making its way down the country and eventually ending up with a booking on the recreation field at Barrow Magna.

Betsy came in very excited, breathless with her news.

'There's a circus coming to Barrow next week. Can we go? There will be animals and clowns and all sorts. Can we go?'

She flopped down in a chair while Annabel, who was mixing one of her potions, looked at her with concern.

'Slow down my girl. What's the rush?'

'Everyone is talking about it. Can we go? Say we can.'

Bit by bit, piece by piece, Annabel extracted the details from her.

'Circus de la Lune. That's a funny name,' she said.

It was coming to Barrow Magna and according to the posters promised an extravagant evening of jugglers, clowns, horseback riding, trapeze artists, elephants, lions and tigers.

Annabel was sceptical about the advertising, but after

consulting Henry, decided that they would all go so that Betsy could see her first proper circus.

The other inhabitants of Happy End were also interested and in the end, Henry was asked to organise a bus to take them all and bring them back. This was nice for Betsy as she would be able to go with her boyfriend Lloyd.

Henry phoned the number given on the posters to make a block booking for the following Saturday night.

The phone was answered by a worried sounding voice, 'Circus de la Lune, Jimmy Jessop here. What can I do for you?'

Henry explained who he was and that he wanted to book a block of seats.

'You had best come over to the site on Tuesday when we get set up. The ticket office will be open then. I'll get our girl to make a note so that you will get what you want.'

The voice sounded more like a proprietor than an employee and Henry, not usually one to put himself forward, said, 'I hope you don't mind me asking, but are you the owner of the circus?'

'That's right lad, Jimmy Jessop, owner, manager and at the moment one worried person. I'll not bother you with the details but it will be a miracle if the show goes on next week I'll tell thee.'

Henry thought that this was a strange conversation to be having on the phone with a stranger and felt prompted to say, 'It there anything we can do to help?'

You could almost hear Jimmy thinking but eventually he

said, 'You sound like a sensible chap, happen it would do me good to talk about it. We are over in Gloucester at the moment but moving over to Barrow Magna the day after tomorrow. Come and have a pint with me at the Crown there this Saturday at about 11 o'clock and I will tell you about it.'

'Right, I will,' said Henry.

When he told Annabel about this, she said, 'He must be a very worried man to talk like that to a complete stranger.'

'Sometimes people will unburden themselves to someone who isn't really involved with them,' said Henry. 'I'll go over on Saturday and see what this is all about.'

When Henry came back home on Saturday Annabel looked at him suspiciously.

'How many pints did you have?' she asked.

'Just three halves,' Henry said cheerfully. 'Let me tell you the story.'

Apparently, Jimmy Jessop had sunk all his money into the circus and, although they were pulling in the crowds wherever they went, the money coming in was only just covering expenses. Expenses were high as Jimmy had to pay for a series of accidents that occurred throughout the tour. These were often things like guy ropes being cut through on the big top the night before a performance, local dogs being found outside the tent with their throats cut, performers' caravans being ransacked and things stolen. On every occasion, it cost Jimmy money to compensate the owners of the animals, to pacify his performers and in the case of the big top to repair the ropes.

'He said it was a mercy that they spotted the damage to the ropes for if they hadn't the whole thing could have collapsed with the audience inside. He also said that if it goes on like this he will have to disband the circus and go back to selling boots. If this happens then Barrow Magna will be their last show.'

Henry leant back and looked quizzically at Annabel.

'What do you think?' he said.

'If you are asking me to get involved, Henry Witchell, you have got another think coming. I know nothing about circuses and don't want to. Its a completely different world.'

Betsy who had been quietly listening to this said, 'There's no harm in finding out a bit more, Mum you're always helping people why not help this man?'

'I'll think about it,' said Annabel, 'But, don't hold out any hopes.'

'I know Mum,' Betsy said to her father later. 'She will help, I know she will.'

Although Annabel was sorry to hear about Jimmy Jessop's problems, he wasn't a member of the village and as she said to herself in bed that night, 'I've got enough to do trying to keep the village on the straight and narrow.'

That night she dreamt that she was a clown in the circus and to her horror the tent above her head started to crumble and come down on the audience. In her dream she could hear screams as the people struggled to get out of the tent. One of the other clowns, a man with a wide smile painted over a mouth that was anything but smiling gave her a push and said, 'Get out quick,' but she found herself unable to move.

She woke with Henry shaking her shoulder.

'Are you all right, love,' he asked.

'Not really,' she said gathering herself together. 'I've just had a dreadful dream; it might have been a premonition. Whatever it was, it tells me that I'm going to have to help Mr Jessop.'

It was now Monday and the circus hands were putting the final touches to the site, as they were to open on Wednesday. On Tuesday they would rehearse and make final preparations.

Henry had phoned Jimmy Jessop and asked if they could come over and look around. 'Unofficially of course.'

'Jimmy laughed and said, 'It won't be unofficial lad, news travels like wildfire in a setup like this.'

It was arranged that Henry and Annabel would take Betsy over to see if she could join the circus as one of the odd job girls who do everything from taking tickets to selling icecream to the audience and help out where ever they are needed. Officially it would be an interview with Jimmy and his head girl Claire Roberts, but it was really to give Annabel a chance to look round.

'But what happens if I get the job?' asked Betsy. 'I know it's the school holidays but I don't think I could do that sort of thing.'

'Don't worry,' said Annabel. 'Jimmy knows why we are there. He will give us a tour of the circus then he will interview you and tell you that you're not suitable.'

In the event, it didn't turn out like that. Jimmy showed them round the circus where everyone was rehearsing. The clowns, without makeup and dressed in shirts and jeans were running around the ring performing somersaults, pretending to empty buckets of whitewash down each other's trousers. Everywhere was a hive of activity. Above their heads, two trapeze artists were performing their act.

'I had no idea that so much preparation went into a performance,' said Annabel.

'It's a question of getting back up to standard,' said Jimmy. 'You see when we strike the tent and move to the next location it takes a few days and especially with the athletic acts, muscles stiffen up and need to be exercised. As you can imagine this is particularly important for the high wire artists and the flyers.' He waved up to the trapeze artists above.

They went around to the animal enclosures where he introduced them to Claire Roberts, a tall fair-haired girl, who was grooming one of the horses.

'Claire is my top girl,' he said. 'Got tired of an office job in Bradford, loved horses and so came to join us.'

Claire turned and smiled at them. She stroked the horse's mane.

'This is Picador,' she said. 'He's my favourite.'

The horse nuzzled her arm.

'I've taken Claire into my confidence,' Jimmy said. 'She knows why you are here.'

'I hope you can help,' she said. 'I love this life as many others here do and we don't want it to end. What we really need is a miracle.'

'That's just what you may get,' said Annabel.

Claire looked puzzled. 'No offence but I can't see how ordinary members of the public can help when we can't find out who is doing this ourselves.'

Jimmy patted her on the shoulder.

'Anything's worth a try,' he said. 'Henry has told me that Mrs Witchell is rather a specialist at this sort of thing.'

Annabel smiled.

'Let's go back to the office,' she said. 'Perhaps we can get down to specifics.'

Betsy lingered behind with Claire.

'My mother's a witch,' she said quietly.

Claire's eyes opened wide but she didn't say anything, just gave a little nod.

Back in the caravan that served as Jimmy's office he went through the list of accidents and mishaps.

'Of course,' he said. 'Some of them are probably genuine. Accidents do happen but this many must be more than coincidence.'

Claire had been quiet up to now but she broke in with, 'I think we ought to employ Betsy as it gives Mrs Witchell a chance to come over and look around.'

'Call me Annabel,' Annabel said. 'And don't be afraid to tell everyone I'm a witch it might put the frighteners into someone.'

Jimmy looked surprised at this but then said to Henry, 'I see what you mean about Annabel being a specialist. Perhaps we do need some special powers.'

Betsy agreed to take up quarters with Claire in her caravan. This was just temporary employment while the circus was in Barrow Magna. It gave Annabel the chance to play the worried mother coming over each day to see how her daughter was settling in.

That night as they sat in front of the fire Henry said, 'It's not the same without Betsy here. I suppose that it will be like this when she really leaves home.'

'She has got to go sometime and if she passes her exams this year she will be off to university if she can get a place.' Annabel smiled at him.

In bed that night Annabel had the same dream. But this time the clown who told her to get out of the tent was much closer. He thrust his face close to hers and she was able to see his features behind the clown's mask.

Next day she set off to the circus. This was the final day before they opened to the public and as usual there was a buzz of activity.

Word about her had obviously gone round as everyone she met looked at her in a funny way.

'They all know you're a witch,' said Jimmy when they met. 'It will be interesting to see if the accidents stop. If we do get anything major then that's the end as far as I am concerned.'

'I'm looking for a particular clown,' said Annabel. 'It

may be he has something to do with this.'

Jimmy took her into the ring where the clowns, this time dressed in their outfits with full makeup, were rehearsing their routines. They stood watching them for a while.

'Every clown has their own special makeup, said Jimmy. 'Which one are you looking for?'

'It's difficult to tell them apart but I'll know him if I see him,' said Annabel.

There was a sudden commotion outside the tent. Claire came running in.

'The tiger's escaped. Someone must have left the cage unlocked.'

'Where's Hugo?' Jimmy asked. He turned to Annabel. 'Hugo is the lion tamer. He looks after the cats.'

'I've tried his caravan but there's no answer,' Claire replied. 'What shall we do?'

Without replying, Annabel was out of the tent in a flash.

The tiger was at the horse enclosure. The stallions were frightened, pawing the ground and trying to get as far away from the beast as possible.

Annabel went straight up to the tiger. It snarled and turned to face her. Fixing it with her eyes, she slowly advanced and patted it on the head. Its snarl turned to a purr and it obediently turned and made its way back to its cage. Two circus hands with sticks quickly jumped in and closed the cage door.

'That was some trick,' said Jimmy who had stood by watching. 'Ah, here's Hugo.'

A large muscular man with a luxurious moustache came up to them rubbing his eyes.

'I'm sorry Jimmy, I must have been asleep. I had a late night last night. The cats were restless and I had to keep coming out to pacify them. What happened?'

'Rajah got out of his cage,' said Jimmy. 'Annabel here got him back in.'

'You're the witch lady,' said Hugo shaking her hand. 'I've heard all about you. I didn't know that lion taming was one of a witch's accomplishments. You must come in with my lions sometime.'

'Hugo is an old fake really,' said Jimmy. 'Most of his lions are quite old and they do anything he tells them for food.'

'Rajah's not like that however, he's still young and dangerous. Who let him out?' asked Hugo.

'Claire spoke up. 'We don't know. I just happened to see he was out and when I couldn't rouse you I panicked and went to see Jimmy. Thank goodness you were here Mrs Witchell.'

Betsy came up at that moment. 'I saw someone by the cages this morning,' she said. 'I didn't get a good look at them, just a back view. I thought it was just one of the hands feeding them.'

'All's well that ends well,' said Jimmy. 'Now you must excuse me, we have a dress rehearsal in half an hour and I have to get changed into my ring master's outfit.'

'I hadn't realised that Jimmy was ring master as well,' said Annabel.

'Yes,' said Claire. 'He loves it, strutting around the ring pretending to be in charge but of course everyone knows exactly what they are doing so really he's not needed.

'And how are you getting on, love,' Annabel said to Betsy.

'It's early days yet but Claire is teaching me an awful lot. I've been out grooming the horses this morning but fortunately had finished by the time Rajah got out.'

There is something very funny going on with that circus,' Annabel told Henry when she got back. 'I've told Betsy to keep her eyes open.'

'Did you find the clown you were looking for,' he asked.

'That's a funny thing,' she said. 'I got distracted by the tiger incident but when I looked at the clowns there was no-one who looked like my clown.'

'Maybe it was just a dream then,' said Henry.

'No, I'm convinced that this man, whoever he is, had something to do with these accidents.'

That night Annabel shut herself away with her crystal ball leaving Henry alone. She spent a long time poring over it but when she came back she had what Henry called her determined look.

'I know what's going to happen and when. It will take place during the show tomorrow night,' she said. 'I think I know how to prevent it, but I'm going to need help.'

She told Henry what she had seen in the crystal and what she wanted him to do.

The next day Henry was out most of the time and when he came back at about teatime he sank into a chair exhausted.

'I've done everything you asked and more,' he said. 'Let's just hope you are right.'

'I'll get going then,' Annabel said. 'See you later. I've left your tea in the kitchen.'

Annabel disliked riding her broomstick before it was dark so she just transported herself to the field outside the circus by magic.

There was the usual hustle and bustle as they prepared for the evening performance. She found Betsy sitting with two other girls waiting to be ice-cream sellers for the evening.

'I need to talk to you alone,' she said.

She took Betsy over to the side of one of the caravans and explained what was going to happen.

'Just keep your eyes and ears open and if you get a message from me get out of the tent quickly and do what I ask.'

Betsy knew what this meant as they had often practiced sending telepathic messages to one another.

'All right, Mum, but take care won't you.'

Annabel smiled, 'It's them as needs to take care you will see,' she said and went off to find Jimmy Jessop.

Half an hour before the show the crowds began to stream in. Claire Roberts was on the ticket desk and nodded to Annabel as she passed into the tent.

Henry was standing by the performer's entrance to the ring looking up.

'It's all set as you asked,' he said. 'I can't believe what you've told me.

Annabel looked grim, 'Just make sure everything goes to plan,' she said.

They went out of the tent and Annabel took him on a tour of the outside of the tent.

'Look here,' she said. 'The guy ropes holding the main supports have been almost cut through on this side. My guess is whoever did it will cut through the ropes on the other side and the whole thing will come crashing down on everyone in the tent. They won't stand a chance.'

As they spoke the last few stragglers entered the tent, the flap was closed, the band struck up and the show began.

Annabel drew Henry back into the shadow of the caravans. They had stationed themselves on the side of the big top where the ropes were still uncut and holding firm.

The show was well under way and Henry was getting cold from waiting when Annabel clutched at his arm.

'Look,' she said, and there amongst the guy ropes was a figure and a flickering light.

Henry came to life immediately. 'Now,' he shouted.

Immediately a ring of powerful torches shone out focussing on the figure among the ropes and the men behind the torches advanced in an ever-closing ring.

After one feeble attempt to escape the menacing circle, the figure gave a moan and collapsed onto the grass, a knife falling from its hand.

Annabel forced her way through the circle and turned the body over shining a torch on its face.

'Well Claire, you led us quite a dance. What made you

think you could get away with this?'

'Keep away from me, all of you,' Claire's face looked evil in the light of the torches. 'Keep away from me.'

Bill Baxter and another man from the village took hold of her and marched her over to Jimmy Jessop's caravan.

'Here's your culprit,' said Annabel.

'I can't believe it,' said Jimmy. 'Why would she want to do all these terrible things.'

Claire struggled in Bill Baxter's grip. 'Because of what you did to my father,' she said.

'Your father? I don't know your father,' he looked puzzled.

'Yes you do,' she said. 'He was one of the Flying Roberts one of the best trapeze artists in the business until you ruined him.'

Annabel sent a thought to Betsy.

Jimmy looked helplessly around. 'What is she talking about,' he said. 'I've never ruined anyone in my life.'

'Yes you did. Instead of employing them, you turned both my mother and father out and after that my father couldn't get a job. He began drinking and that was his ruin. When my mother died I lost touch with him. He wandered off somewhere and I never saw him again. Let me go, let me go.'

Claire struggled in Bill's arms and collapsed on to the settee.

Jimmy sat down still looking puzzled.

'I still don't know what this is about,' he said. 'I remember an act I tried out when we were first recruiting, I can't remember their names, but the man was so drunk he couldn't even climb the ladder to the first trapeze. There was no way I was going to employ them.'

Annabel then took charge. Everyone had crowded into Jimmy Jessop's caravan so she sent them out, all except for Jimmy, Claire and Henry. She went outside and thanked everyone who had come from the village to help.

'Get them back on the bus, Bill,' she said. 'Then call in at the Fox's Revenge. Jimmy Jessop has arranged for everyone to have a pint on him. Richard, the landlord knows all about it.'

'I don't know if the Reverend Harding will have a pint,' Bill said to Annabel as he passed. 'But the rest of us certainly will. Thanks Annabel, a good night's work.'

At that moment Betsy arrived with a man dressed in a clown's costume hastily wiping off his clown's makeup.

As they entered the caravan Claire looked up.

'Father,' she cried. The man took her in his arms.

'I think I owe you an explanation,' he said to Jimmy. 'I'm Jack Roberts, Claire's father. You were quite right to turn me down when I came to you for work. I was drinking heavily and was good for nothing. It wasn't until your mother died Claire that I was brought to my senses. I applied for a job as a clown with this circus using another name.

'Jimmy Jessop is a good man and a good employer. I knew you were with the circus and wanted to be near you but I hid behind a clown's mask.'

'But I took the job to avenge you,' Claire cried. 'I thought it was all his fault.'

'Father and daughter reunited and the mysterious accidents explained,' said Annabel afterwards. 'Not a bad piece of work.'

'But what will happen to Claire?' asked Betsy. 'They will have to call the police in.'

'I'm not so sure,' said Henry. 'Circus folk have a tradition of dealing with their own problems. I don't think we shall hear any more about it. In any event, Jimmy Jessop is happy and Circus de la Lune is saved. Let's go and enjoy the Saturday night performance.'

And they did.

13

All that glitters

It was the summer holiday and Betsy had just received her exam results.

'I've passed, I've passed,' she jumped up and down hugging Annabel and Henry.

'Then, its university for you next year,' said Annabel.

'If they will have me,' said Betsy still jumping up and down. 'The school helped us with the application forms so we shall just have to wait and see.'

'Everything seems to be happening this week,' said Annabel. 'You passing your exams, then Bill Baxter finds a gold amulet on the hillside and now a strange character turning up in the village.'

Two days before, Bill had been using his metal detector on Barrow Hill. He was always doing this in different places around the village, for as he said in the pub, someone somewhere is going to have hidden something valuable in the ground and I'm going to be the one to find it.

Of course Bill was thinking of the Romans who had occupied the area and of the barrow that lay under the hill hence its name. Fortunately he didn't think of digging indiscriminately in the hill as he would have got more than he bargained for.

Everyone in the village, except perhaps Annabel held Barrow Hill in awe as it was well known that fairies lived under the hill. No one wanted to upset them as they could play nasty tricks on anyone who disturbed them.

Bill was running his metal detector over a wooded area on the hill when he got a massive reading on the meter. Digging down with the trowel he always carried with him he came across what he thought was a necklace encrusted in dirt. When he got it home and cleaned it up it turned out to be a circlet of dull yellow metal. He hoped it was gold and the first person he showed it to, the Reverend Alistair Harding, agreed.

'You ought to take it to Cirencester Museum, Bill,' he said. 'They can tell you more about it. They can probably tell you its value and let you know the proper procedure to deal with it.'

'Would you keep it for me vicar until I decide,' he said.

Alistair Harding was reluctant to keep such a potentially valuable item in his house but he said he would.

'I think you will have to declare it to the police,' he said.

'Won't they prosecute me for hunting for it?' Bill asked.

'I was trespassing on the hill.'

'No-one owns the hill Bill, its common land so that shouldn't be any problem. The problem might be very different. You see, if it is what we might call fairy gold then we need to talk to Mrs Witchell to ask her advice.

The next day Alistair Harding went to see Annabel.

It was a fine day and Annabel and Betsy were out in the Garden Centre with Henry when Alistair arrived with the golden amulet.

'Annabel greeted him with, 'So you want to know if its fairy gold?'

'Well, I … how did you know?' he asked.

Annabel chuckled, 'That's not witchery vicar. You ought to know by now that news travels fast in Happy End.'

Alistair was just about to open the bag he was carrying when Annabel stopped him.

'No call to show this to everyone,' she said. 'Come inside and have a cup of tea.'

There were one or two people in the garden centre looking at the plants and Annabel noticed that one of them looked like the tramp that had recently turned up in the village.

As they went into the house she noticed that the tramp was now talking to Betsy.

'Betsy, can you come in a minute,' she called.

Betsy obediently came into the house.

'Would you make a cup of tea for us, love. The vicar has brought something to show us.'

Betsy went off into the kitchen and Alistair took the amulet out of his bag and handed it to Annabel.

She turned it over slowly. As she held it to the light a shadow passed over the window. She turned quickly but there was no-one there.

'I believe Bill found it on the hill,' she said. 'It's pretty certainly gold and fairy gold at that. Best thing he could do is put it back but knowing him I don't suppose he will.'

'I'll tell him that,' said Alistair, 'but he has asked me to keep it for him while he thinks about it.'

'Better keep it safe then vicar, for there's them that might steal it and not only those of human persuasion.'

Alistair suddenly felt a chill in his bones.

'As though someone had walked over my grave,' he said to his wife afterwards.

Fortunately, he had a small safe in his study and was able to put the amulet in by squashing his papers up together.

Meanwhile Annabel was doing some investigating. The tramp she had seen in the garden centre had taken up residence in the old barn down by Mr Heathcote's cottage.

Annabel visited Tom Heathcote the next day, taking him some scones she had baked that morning.

'Thank you kindly,' he said. 'It's not often young ladies come to see me these days bearing gifts like these. Will you stay and have one with me and maybe a cup of tea or something stronger?'

'A cup of tea will do nicely, Tom,' she said and when Tom had come back with a cracked teapot and two delicate china cups she asked, 'I've come to ask you about the person you've got sleeping in your barn.'

'He's all right,' said Tom. 'I know he looks like a tramp but I reckon he's a gentleman down on his luck. He's paid me for staying in barn and he's no trouble. Mind you the coins he paid me in are a bit strange. He must come from foreign parts, I reckon.'

He went over to a drawer, took out a small handful of coins and put them in front of Annabel.

'That's what he paid me with. What do you think I should do with them?'

Annabel took one and turned it over. As she did so she saw in her mind's eye the figure of a man, not a tramp but a terrifying, commanding figure. The figure beckoned to her.

'Are you all right, lass,' Tom Heathcote asked.

Annabel shook herself.

'I'm fine,' she said. 'These coins are gold Tom and probably worth quite a bit. You should get them valued. Picket, the Jeweller in Barrow is an honest man. Take them in to him and let him have a look at them.'

As soon as she could reasonably get away she left Tom looking with wonder at the coins. Her path took her past the old barn and she knew immediately that she was going to meet the stranger.

He stood there square in her path. He had changed from his tramps disguise and towered over Annabel, resplendent in fairy finery and she knew at once that he was King of the Fairies.

'I'm here to recover the gold that is ours.' he said.

'I know,' said Annabel. 'At the moment it's locked in the vicar's safe. Why can't you just take it from there?'

'There are certain laws in the universe,' he said. 'I am forbidden to approach a holy man and in any case the gold must be given freely. In the meantime I shall take a hostage who will be returned once the gold is handed over to us.'

He vanished leaving Annabel alone.

'I wonder what he meant about a hostage,' Annabel said to Henry when she arrived back home.

'I must go to see the vicar to arrange to give the gold back.'

'How will you give it back,' asked Henry. 'Did he tell you how to do it?'

'No, but it will arrange itself,' said Annabel.

It wasn't until later that they realised that Betsy was missing. Annabel had gone over to the Rectory to see Alistair who was only too willing to hand the amulet over to Annabel once the situation had been explained to him.

'The sooner it goes back where it belongs, the better but hadn't you better tell Bill?'

'You're right,' she said. 'First I must put this in a safe place.'

When she arrived back home, Henry was hunting through the house.

'I can't find Betsy,' he said. 'The last I saw of her was in the garden centre talking to that tramp who keeps hanging about.'

'So that's what he meant about a hostage,' thought Annabel. 'Well we can soon stop that.'

She told Henry what she thought had happened, then, taking the amulet she set off for Barrow Hill.

Before she left Henry asked, 'Will Betsy be all right? Will any harm come to her?'

'She will be all right. The Fairy King rules his kingdom and his Queen with a rod of iron, everything will be fine.'

When she reached the copse of trees on the hill, as she expected, the Fairy King was waiting for her. Silently she handed him the amulet. He took it, nodded slightly and vanished.

'What about Betsy?' she called.

The King reappeared.

'You have a lovely daughter,' he said. 'We decided to keep her for a while to instruct her in our ways.'

'That wasn't the agreement,' said Annabel

'Nevertheless, that is what we have decided,' he said and turning away from her vanished into the trees.

Annabel returned home with a heavy heart. She knew that her powers were no match for fairy magic and so didn't even think of challenging the King's decision. She needed to think about what they could do to get their daughter back.

But that's another story!